Aunt Harriet and Me

Our Life in the Boarding House

by

Geraldine Sylvester

For Laurie Sonny & My
dear Aunt —
With Love .
Gerry

DORRANCE PUBLISHING CO., INC.
PITTSBURGH, PENNSYLVANIA 15222

Dedication

To Barbara Rouleau and Marilyn Janelle.
    For no other reason than I have been blessed to have them embrace me as a friend for more than sixty-five years, and that has been one mighty long time.

ISBN: 978-1-4349-0838-4
eISBN: 978-1-4349-5592-0

Printed in the United States of America

First Printing

For more information or to order additional books, please contact:
Dorrance Publishing Co., Inc.
701 Smithfield Street
Pittsburgh, Pennsylvania 15222
U.S.A.
1-800-788-7654
www.dorrancebookstore.com

Preface

This story takes place at a time when boardinghouses were a real basic part of American culture. Many of them were once the large homes of well-to-do people, but poor economic conditions after the Depression forced many of their current owners to rent out rooms. Many boardinghouse owners also provided good, nourishing meals. These were places where single people from all walks of life, immigrants who came to find the "American dream," married couples, and even families had safe places to live, oftentimes with the families sharing a single room and even with all the children sleeping three or more in a single bed. They were homes where friendships and extended families developed and where people could feel a sense of dignity, because there were no handouts, no freebies, and everyone had to pay his fair share. Prevalent in the larger cities like New York, Boston, and Chicago, boardinghouses also could be found in just about every small town.

It was a time before the government built the massive public housing projects that dotted our landscape, a time when such surplus foods as butter, large blocks of cheese, beans, rice, flour, and cans of "mystery meats" were provided to those who were deemed qualified. Many folks took advantage of the program and used this food to feed their families, and others just took it all even if they didn't intend to use it. They took it because it was free and they felt they were entitled to it. When the waste of the surplus food program was recognized, it was replaced by government-issued food stamps. Again some used the stamps wisely, and others sold them at a discount for cash or found grocers who were willing to let them be used not for baby formula and family foods, but for beer, wine, and cigarettes. All of this, plus the fact that after the war people were becoming committed to owning a home of their own, led to a decline in the number of boardinghouses. Unfortunately, today's economic downturn sees an upswing in boardinghouses again.

In *Aunt Harriet and Me,* the boardinghouse is fictional, but we learn what life was like from the main character, a young girl who spent many of her growing-up years as a boarder. She lived there with her aunt, uncle, and a variety of other fictional characters. Even though these are made-up people, I suspect that as you read along, you'll stop at least once or maybe twice and think, "Oh, my God, I knew someone just like that."

I also claim that the small town where the boardinghouse is located is fictional, but there sure are events, scenes, and everyday happenings that are reminiscent of the town where I grew up. Who knows? Maybe there isn't any such thing as pure fiction; every thought or idea has to come from somewhere. My hope, however, is that you'll enjoy this read regardless of how much is real and how much is from outer space.

Thanks

There are always so many people to thank. Foremost among them are:

My kids, who encourage me no matter what I attempt. It doesn't matter if it's a big project, a little project, or some crazy idea; they are always there for me.

My husband, Bob, who should certainly be thanked for putting up with me for more than forty-two years. He is a real gem.

And my friend Susan Novak, who keeps me on the straight and narrow. She reminds me of such things as periods and commas that need to go where I put all those dashes and dots. She puts quotation marks in the right places, corrects the things I put in Capital Letters that really don't need to be, makes sure I don't change tenses in the middle of a sentence, and also creates paragraphs out of my rambling stories. She was there for me through *Windy Hill, The Reluctant Innkeeper,* and now *Aunt Harriet and Me: Our Life in the Boardinghouse.* She is not only bright; she is also damned patient and a good friend.

A Big House in a Small Mill Town

The house I lived in wasn't always a boardinghouse. Years ago it was a beautiful family home built by the same people who came to town to build the mills. It was a big, rambling place with three floors, a large wraparound porch, and an attached barn. It was the kind of place you would expect to be built on acres of land, off by itself on a country road. It wasn't. It was right there in the middle of town three times the size of any other house for miles around.

There wasn't much lawn in the front, just small strips of grass that abutted the sidewalk. To one side, the grass went on for a good distance until it reached the small railroad depot. I wondered which came first, the house or the depot, but was never told. Maybe people couldn't remember, or I guess it didn't matter much.

There was a large lake right in back, but between the house and the lake were the railroad tracks. They didn't spoil the view or really cause any problems. If you wanted to swim or fish, you just had to cross over those tracks, climb down the banking, and there you were. The only time you thought about how close the tracks were was when a train went by, and then the house shook a little.

The house was painted white with black shutters, just like about every other house in town, but, of course, it had about a bazillion more shutters. When the family lived there, flowers were planted all around the porch, and pots of flowers sat on the railing. On Sundays when people were out riding around, they used to come through town just to gawk at what they called the Mill House.

But when I lived there, it didn't look quite like that anymore. It was a weather-beaten, kind of gray color, and many of the shutters were hanging loose or missing altogether. The only flowers were the dandelions that filled the space between the house and the depot. There was one other thing that made it different: the sign that hung off the porch that read, Mrs. W's Place. When people drove by on Sundays, it was not to ooh and ah, but to say to one another, "My God, look at that place. What a shame." But it didn't matter; I loved it. I lived there with my Aunt Harriet, Uncle Ben, and a bunch of other people I thought of as my family. It was my home since I was three years old.

The town was quite small; everybody knew everybody and knew everybody else's business—a town with no secrets, or almost none. There was a filling station right across the street from Mrs. W's with one gas pump. I guess that's all that was needed because not too many people in town had cars of their own. Inside you could buy a cold drink and a pack of cigarettes but not much else. If you wanted a few more groceries, like milk, bread, or canned goods, you went to the grocery store just down the street a little bit, and you could even pay for things later if you didn't have the money on you. But if you really wanted to shop at a big store, you had to get someone to take you eight miles away.

On Saturday mornings you could see the people who had cars heading out of town with friends riding along. Sometimes they'd be gone for the whole day because they'd need other things besides groceries, things they couldn't get here in town—things like needles and thread, underwear, toothbrushes. Lots of things. Those who didn't have friends to take them hopped on the train.

We had good schools. People said they were the best around. The small grammar school sat on a hill and had a lot of land around it. There wasn't any equipment for the playground. Mostly we played jump rope, hopscotch, marbles, and dodge ball, so we didn't need swings or slides or stuff like that. In the winter when we had to find other things to do, we would make snowmen, igloos, and angels in the snow. Sometimes the teachers would flood a low spot in the back, and when the weather was just right, we'd have ice to skate on. The skating wasn't very good because the ice was always really bumpy with grass, dirt, and stuff sticking up, but we skated anyway.

In our school each teacher had three grades to a room, and the older kids had to help the younger ones learn their lessons. In the town that had the big stores, it also had a big school where each teacher had only one grade to teach, but it really didn't make the kids learn any better. That school had a lot of stuff on the playground, but the kids there didn't have any more fun than we did. In fact, at recess there would always be fights about whose turn it was on some old swing or something. We never had to fight about whose turn it was at jumping rope; anyone who wanted to jump just stood in line. The big school also had a cafeteria where kids could buy hot lunches. Everyone said the lunches were pretty bad, so we were glad we didn't have anything fancy like a cafeteria. We were happy just swapping whatever we had packed in our brown bags.

Our high school was just down the road a little bit. It wasn't as big as the grammar school. It probably didn't need to be, because not everyone went there after making it through the eighth grade. There was a gym for basketball games, dances, and big school assemblies. There was a woodworking shop for the boys, a big kitchen so that the girls could learn how to cook, and a couple of sewing machines in case anyone wanted to make a broomstick skirt or apron or some other easy thing.

Every day, first thing in the morning, the girls in cooking class cooked up something that all the high school kids could eat for lunch. It was mostly stuff like beef stew, macaroni and cheese, and American chop suey, but it always tasted really good, and it was free. Whatever the kids didn't eat the teacher just took home to her family. She said it was also her job to teach the girls that it was a sin to waste anything.

The parents in town all chipped in to buy the balls and bats and whatever else was needed so that the school could have some teams. Our teams were really good; they were always winning everything, especially the girls teams. They used to count on my friend Della's father when they had to go out of town for a game. He had a big old truck with benches in the back. He'd just pull up in front of the high school, everyone would pile in, and off they'd go. A couple of times, he forgot to show up; I guess he was probably drunk or something. But nobody wanted to say anything. After all, it was only a couple of times, and nobody else in town had a truck with benches.

Graduation was a big affair. They lined the gym with rows of folding chairs, dragged in a piano so that they could play that march thing, and almost everyone in town showed up. The kids from the grammar school always sang a couple of songs—usually the same ones, and sometimes they didn't sing too well, but it was what everyone expected. The teachers passed out prizes, and one of the kids who was graduating always made a speech about growing up, going out into the world, and stuff like that. At the big school in the neighboring town, they always invited some big shot to come and speak at graduation. We did that only once. We didn't need an outsider, and besides, the one time some man came, nobody could even remember who he was or what he'd said.

After the real program was over, the boys would jump off the stage, fold up some of the chairs, and stack them out in the hall. When there was enough room, the kids and teachers would stand in a long line, and the parents and everyone else walked by to shake their hands. Even the teachers from the grammar school stood in line. And one time when there was a really big class of sixteen graduates, it seemed as though it took forever. Then they would bring up big platters of sandwiches that the cooking class had made, along with brownies, cookies, punch, and other stuff, and everyone would eat. Sometimes townspeople came just for the lunch.

Graduation was sure a special time, and it seemed as though the teachers were even prouder than the parents were. That probably was because they knew the kids really well. Some knew the kids even better than the parents did. Every teacher knew every kid's name. The teachers knew the students' mothers and fathers, their uncles and aunts, and had taught some of their brothers and sisters. But the most unbelievable thing of all was that they seemed to know just how much each kid could do, asked only that everyone do his best, and then helped each one of them do it. I guess that's one big reason why our schools were the best around.

We had a big old grange hall where most all of the town affairs took place. Once in a while on a Saturday, they would show a silent movie. It cost only a nickel to get in, but you had to bring your own popcorn. Folks in town who weren't allowed to use the church basement because they never went to church used the grange hall for weddings and big after-funeral parties. Sometimes I thought that when I got older, I'd like to join the grange. Members had regular meetings and bake sales and did a lot of neat things. I was a little afraid, however, that I wouldn't be able to remember my secret password, so I decided I probably wouldn't join after all.

There were two churches in town, both of them pretty small. The only thing I can tell you about the Protestant church was that it was brown on the outside. I'd never seen the inside because Catholic kids were told never to go in. In fact, my friend Little Mary Theresa told me I should make the sign of the cross whenever I walked by. She said it was just like holding your breath when you ran through a cemetery. It kept out the evil spirits. I wasn't sure how true that was, but I never dared to pass by without crossing myself.

My church was a pretty little white building that sat on a knoll at the other end of town. It was clean as a whistle, and there was always fresh water in the little containers up by the door so that we could bless ourselves as we entered. I guess they thought that if you were blessed, you wouldn't be thinking about how hard the pews were. Downstairs was a big old basement where they put on bean suppers. People who went to church and put their money in the basket could use the basement to have any kind of party they wanted to have. The altar had nice white, starched, embroidered cloths that covered it and stretched way down the sides. There were always flowers of some kind. In the winter they weren't real flowers—just fake—but they were always there to make the place look pretty. And we had a lot of different old priests.

I guess old priests were sent our way because they were too old to tend to big bunches of people. Even though they needed a lot of help around the church, people were willing to pitch in, and everybody seemed to like most of them. Once in a while, when one of our old priests went away to a home or died or something, we'd get to share a young one from the neighboring town.

The town that had the big stores and the big schools also had a really big church, and people in that church always got their own way. When we had to share the priest, we'd have church at seven o'clock in the morning. That gave him time to do us first, have some breakfast, and get back where he came from so that he could do the others at a regular time. I heard some folks complain that it was like going to church in the middle of the night, but they always went. I guess they knew it was a sin not to, and besides, it never lasted very long. Pretty soon they'd find another old one to send our way. That always made everyone happy. It didn't matter how old they were, or how cranky, and even though they all wore the same dresses and said the same prayers in Latin, it was still a good thing to have one of our own. Besides, we didn't have to get up so early.

The mill itself was about two miles out of town, and the people who built the mill also built a dozen little houses really close by for some of their workers. Other workers who didn't live in those houses or who didn't have a car—and most didn't—had to walk the whole way to work. They were the ones who gave the little houses the nickname the Dirty Dozen. It must have been because they were jealous about having to walk so far, because those houses really weren't dirty, at least not at first.

Most all the men in town worked at the mill, and so did some of the women. My aunt told me that just a few years earlier, even kids worked there—little kids, kids so little that they had to stand on stools to reach their machines. Then somebody made a law that said the mill couldn't hire kids anymore. I guess that was because so many of them had accidents. Besides, I don't know how any little kid could work the way my Uncle Ben did. He left early in the morning and came home just in time for supper. He also was one of the walkers, so, man, did he ever get tired. I asked him one time if he wished he lived in one of those Dirty Dozen houses so that he'd be really close, but all he said was "Nope, the boardinghouse is just fine with me." I was glad, because it sure was fine with me.

Many Floors, Many Rooms, Many Characters

I loved the big old kitchen. It had three iceboxes, and sometimes I'd just sit there and watch the drips from the ice hit the pans underneath. There was a great big stove that worked pretty well most of the time and a wooden table with big dark rings where Mrs. Walden had put down hot pots and pans. The floor was covered with brown linoleum that used to have some kind of yellow flowers on it. Most of those were worn off, but in some spots you could still see one or two of them if you tried real hard. In other spots you could see right down to the bare floor. The walls were painted a mustard-color yellow. Uncle Ben called that color "shit brindle." Every spring Mrs. Walden said she was going to paint them some other color, but she never did, at least not while I lived there.

The dining room was just opposite the kitchen on the back side of the house, with windows that faced the railroad tracks. There wasn't much in the dining room: a couple of big old closets that held the dishes and silverware, and a mighty long table. There were only two chairs, one at each end of the table. The chair at the head of the table was for Mrs. Walden in case she had to jump up and get something from the kitchen. The other chair was where Emma, a crabby old boarder, sat most of the time. She used to come to supper really early just so that she could grab that chair. The rest of us—at that time, Kathy, Willy, Sam, Buster, Charlie, Sadie, Shakespeare, Aunt Harriet, Uncle Ben, and me—sat on long benches. It was the only way we could all fit around the table at the same time.

No one ever complained about the food, except for the one time that Kathy, a helper for Mrs. Walden, did the cooking. We always had beans, hot dogs, and homemade brown bread on Saturdays, and once in a while there would be a plateful of pickled tripe. Willy, Sam, and Buster really ate that stuff up, but I sure never did. On Sundays there was always something special like a big old roast of some kind or a ham cooked in a pot with potatoes and green beans. And there was always dessert. One time we even had cream puffs, but Mrs. Walden said they were just too damned hard to make, so mostly we had cakes or pudding.

The parlor was the biggest room of all. It ran the whole length of the front of the house and had the most stuff in it. There were two love seats with curved wood on the backs, arms, and legs. Hardly anyone ever sat on them, so they still looked pretty good. There was a big sofa that might have been fun to sit on if it hadn't been covered with cloth that was kind of itchy and smelled like old cigar smoke. Willy and Sam were the only ones who ever sat there, but I guess if you drink a lot of beer, you don't notice itchy and smelly very much. There were a lot of chairs scattered here and there—puffy, comfortable things—and you could even lean way back in a couple of them.

At the end of the room in front of what used to be a fire-place, Mrs. Walden built shelves for a lot of books. She thought it was a good idea since we couldn't use the fireplace anymore. Those shelves helped bock the drafts and kept the chipmunks from getting in and running all over the place. Hardly anyone ever read the books except Charlie. He'd read every one of them more than once, before he found his own books in the town dump. Buster might have read them if he hadn't been blind, but Emma said they were all stupid books, nothing there that would interest her.

On one side next to the shelves was a card table with four chairs, and underneath were boxes and boxes of puzzles. Nobody ever tried to put them together, probably because most of them had pieces missing. On the other side was a big built-in bin where a whole lot of wood was kept. I'm not sure why we still kept the bin full of wood since we couldn't use the fireplace anymore, but there it was. Emma also thought that was stupid, and probably that time she was right.

I didn't spend much time in the parlor, because Emma was always plunked there, and she didn't like me very much. But then Emma hardly liked anybody, even Emma. She'd sit all day long in the best chair and watch the people walk by. Sometimes I'd just peek at her from the hallway. I thought she might have been pretty once. She had nice silver-colored hair that she wore in tiny tight waves. She went down the street every Friday morning to get a lady to wave it for her, and even though it looked the same, she'd always complain that the lady did a better job the week before. Then she'd go on ranting and raving about how nice her hair had been when she was younger and how it was a pretty red color. She sure was proud of that. She had an okay face, even though there were wrinkles all over the place, but I doubt she got very many of them from smiling. Her eyes, which were hazel, never sparkled the way my aunt's did; they just kind of snapped. She was a thin lady with big boobs that looked as if they might make her back ache to carry them around, but she was kind of proud of them, as well. All in all, she wasn't bad looking. Nobody could really call her ugly, at least not on the outside. But if what my aunt said was true, "Pretty is as pretty does," then sure as the dickens nobody could call her pretty, either. Peeking in on her as she watched the people go by, I could hear her mumble things like "Boy, she sure got fat" or "Why isn't that lazy man working today?" or "How many more kids is that one going to have?" And when a lady named Esther walked by, she said, "If she wasn't the sheriff's girlfriend, she'd be in jail." Most didn't pay much attention to Emma's mumblings, 'cause as I said, she hardly liked anybody, and hardly anybody liked her. So I guess it was fair in the long run.

Even though there were three floors, nobody ever went all the way up. Mrs. Walden always kept the door to that third floor locked. I think that's where she probably threw all the stuff that had belonged to her lousy husband once he finally died. Sometimes I was just itching to get up there and have a look around. Other times I was scared just walking by the stairwell. I thought not only was Old Man Walden's stuff up there, but his ghost was up there, as well, just wandering around. Sometimes at night when I couldn't get to sleep, I'd hear him walking back and forth.

All of the boarders' bedrooms were on the second floor, but Mrs. Walden had a room right in back of the kitchen. She told me she stayed there because she had to get up early to cook breakfast. I think she really stayed there so that she could keep her eye on the comings and goings of Willy and Sam, 'cause they sure did need watching.

There were eight bedrooms on the second floor, all pretty much the same size except for a couple. Mine was really tiny. I had a cot for a bed, a little rocking chair, and a kid's table and chair set. The set used to have four chairs, but we could fit in only one. That was okay 'cause I was the only kid anyway. There wasn't any closet, but before I got the table and chair, there was a bureau for all my clothes. Aunt Harriet moved the bureau into her room, and even though it made it pretty crowded, she thought that if I had a little table to play on, it would keep me from hanging out in the kitchen so much. That really didn't work, because my room was dreary without a window or people around. Besides, if I was there all by myself, I could hear Old Man Walden loud and clear, even if it wasn't nighttime.

My room was right next to Aunt Harriet and Uncle Ben's with a door in between, so I guess it was a suite. At least that's what Emma said it was. She used to complain about it, telling me I was spoiled, always had to have the best. That was kind of funny because I thought her room was really the best, and our suite was probably only second best.

I loved the big windows in my aunt's room. There were two of them that looked out on the railroad tracks and the lake beyond. There was a big old iron bed, three bureaus crowded together, a couple of little tables for lamps and Uncle Ben's radio, and two chairs. One of those chairs was hard as a rock, so we didn't really sit on it— just used it to pile stuff on. There were also some other nice things.

My Aunt Harriet had hung a mirror over one of the bureaus, and over the bed she had hung a picture of two little kids crossing a bridge with their guardian angel watching over them. The cover on the bed was made of a bazillion little patches, all different shapes and colors. I always had to take my shoes off when I wanted to lie down on that big old bed, because Aunt Harriet had made that cover a few years before and it was still in pretty good shape. She always was very careful about things, and so was Uncle Ben, but mostly he was careful about his money. Whenever I lay down there, I'd make believe the guardian angel was watching me, too, and I would always take great big sniffs so that I could smell my aunt's dusting powder. If I closed my eyes, I could pretend the room was filled with lilacs. I loved being in that room almost as much as I loved being in the kitchen, and that's where I'd go whenever Kathy or Mrs. Walden told me I was "under foot." When Mrs. Walden told me, she always did it in a nice way, but Kathy just used to shout, "Get the hell out of this kitchen!" One time she even pushed me, but my aunt made sure that never happened again.

Emma's room was on the corner and quite a bit bigger than all the others. It had a small fireplace that couldn't be used, either, but Mrs. Walden had blocked this one off with a wardrobe kind of thing instead of bookshelves. Of course, Emma thought it was ugly and was always asking Mrs. Walden to do something different, but she never did. There was a bed with four big posts, a comfortable rocking chair, and a nice bureau, but best of all were the four windows to let in a lot of extra sunshine. It was the room Emma insisted on having, probably because it used to be the room the mill boss and his wife had when they lived there. But in the summer she'd complain that there was too much sun, and in the winter she said she got all the drafts. In the fall she hated to have to look at everything dying, and in the spring all she could see out of those damned windows was mud, mud, mud. Every morning she gave us a running report on how bad things were according to the season. Emma was like that.

Kathy's room was right next to mine. She didn't pay to live there—just helped Mrs. Walden with the chores to cover her room and board. But one time I heard Mrs. Walden mumble that Kathy was more trouble than she was worth. I guess that was because she often did strange things. One time she moved all the furniture into the middle of the parlor 'cause she wanted to vacuum really well, but then she refused to put it back. And one week when it was time to change the sheets, she just took the dirty sheets from one bed and put them on another and hid the clean ones. It wasn't until after supper that Mrs. Walden realized she didn't have any dirty sheets to wash and knew something was up. It took her forever to get Kathy to tell her where she had hidden all the clean ones. If Aunt Harriet hadn't pitched in, we wouldn't have gotten to bed until after midnight. I sure was glad it got all straightened out. I wouldn't have wanted to sleep in Willy's or Sam's sheets, but it would have been funny if Emma had to. Oh, my gosh, would that have been funny!

You could never guess what Kathy's room would look like.

She kept changing things around, even the furniture. One time she put her bed so close to the door that I could hardly get in. I guess she must have done what I had to do: open the door as far as it would go and then crawl across the bed to get to the other side. It wasn't really anything to be concerned about, because in a few days she'd just push the stuff somewhere else. There wasn't much you could do with a bed, a bureau, and two chairs in a small room, but she was always trying to make it look different.

She pretended she had secret things in there that nobody knew about, but I doubted it. Her walls were always covered with something or other. First she had umpteen old postcards from different places. She said she'd been to all of them, but I doubted that, as well. I doubted Kathy had ever been to Paris or Egypt, but I sure never dared to say anything about not believing her. After a while she'd take down all the postcards and plaster her wall with pictures she drew. They were pretty bad pictures, but she said she got them from her dreams. Next thing you knew, she'd hang pictures of cars or bicycles or buses that she'd cut from some old magazine. One time she had nothing on her walls but funky old maps. Then she'd start all over again—first the postcards, then the pictures, right on down the line. I sure didn't understand it. I guess I thought the whole thing was kind of stupid. But my aunt understood; she explained to me it was just a sign that Kathy wished she could move on, go to different places, see different things. She wasn't sure just where Kathy had come from but was pretty sure she'd probably never be able to go to any of those places in her dreams. My aunt tried never to say bad things about people. Once in a while she'd slip when it came to Emma, but all she said to me about Kathy was that "she had limitations." After she explained it a little, I didn't think what Kathy did to her room was stupid anymore, just kind of sad.

On the other side of the hall, the room way at the end was where Sadie and Shakespeare lived. That wasn't his real name, but that's what everyone called him, even Sadie. They looked just alike: short, very round, and very different from most folks I knew. I thought they were brother and sister, but they weren't. They were husband and wife. Sometimes, hand in hand, they would hitchhike eight miles to the neighboring town to buy a bottle of beer for Shakespeare and a little bag of candy for Sadie. They'd hitch back, enjoy their treats, and then an hour or so later do it all over again—sometimes three or four times a day, except in the winter, when they'd call the cab. They never gave anybody any trouble; they just kind of hung on to each other. Mrs. Walden didn't mind having them there. She just said, "Their elevator doesn't go to the top floor."

The only thing special about their room was the feather bed. Every night they'd fluff it up, over and over again, just to make sure one of them hadn't put a dent in it somewhere. There weren't any pictures of angels on the wall or a mirror or anything like that, but they did have a lot of other things scattered about. Shakespeare liked cigar boxes. Even though he never smoked a cigar, he had them all over the place. I guess he used them to save special things in. One time I asked Sadie how old she was, and she told me she didn't know, "because Shakespeare keeps all the papers." I guess if I ever really wanted to know I would probably have to look through all those cigar boxes.

There was a big basket at the foot of the bed where Sadie kept her treasures and souvenirs. She had some junky pins and beads that she never wore, a bunch of keys that wouldn't open anything, a menu from one time they ate out, and a whole bunch of other stuff, including some Popsicle sticks. I'm not sure how much she really cared about the stuff in the basket, but she had a doll that she sure did love. It was an old raggedy rag doll that she slept with, and she loved it so much she even brought it to the supper table. The only time she didn't have the doll with her was when she was hitching back and forth to get her candy. I thought it was really funny that she called her doll Mama, so one time I asked her why she didn't name her Baby instead of Mama. Boy, did she ever get upset, I mean really upset! She hugged that doll and cried, "Mama, Mama," over and over. It took my Aunt Harriet to calm her down and then to tell me I should learn to mind my own business. I didn't care; I still thought Baby was a much better name, so when I'd see Sadie with her doll, I'd just say to myself, but not out loud, "There go Sadie and Baby."

Next to them was Buster. He never got in anyone's way, and we didn't get in his way, 'cause he was blind as a bat. I thought he was kind and gentle, but I guess he hadn't always been like that.

Aunt Harriett told me that when he was a young kid, he was nasty and mean. Growing up, he lived with his mother, father, and an old, blind grandmother. He used to tease her and taunt her—run around her chair and either pull her hair or smack her and then run out of reach. "Buster," she'd say, "someday you'll be sorry." She told him that over and over again: "Buster, someday you'll be sorry." And the very day she died, Buster went blind. I knew if my aunt told me that, it had to be true, so I decided never to make fun of someone who couldn't see, couldn't hear, was funny looking, or was big and fat—or anything.

Buster didn't have a lot of things around his room, probably so that there wouldn't be much for him to bump into. He did have two buckets of change, a hook to hang his cane on, and his very own radio. But mostly that was it. There weren't any pictures or stuff like that, 'cause he couldn't have seen them anyway. I used to like seeing those buckets of change stacked side by side. Every month when Mrs. Walden cashed his checks, and after she took what was her due, she'd give him big bags of change. Feeling the coins was the only way Buster could tell what was what. But one day Mrs. Walden had a brainstorm. She brought back paper money and cut one little corner off the one-dollar bills, two corners off the fives, and put a little cut on the top of the ten-dollar ones. That way Buster could tell the paper ones apart and Mrs. Walden wouldn't have to be lugging around all that heavy change. It worked pretty well, except Buster still wanted change, so one month he'd get paper and the next month he'd get the coins. That was what was decided after Mrs. Walden and Buster had a long and loud kind of talk.

He had other ways of telling things apart. Any two things that were close in size and shape he'd find a way to mark. He put two strips of tape on his tube of toothpaste so that he wouldn't brush his teeth with the greasy stuff he used to make his hair shiny. And he taped a button on the top of his horse liniment so that he would- n't get it mixed up with his Listerine. He was very clever that way, and he also kept his room neat and his bed made nice and smooth. He sure was different from either Willy or Sam. They hardly ever made their beds, their clothes were all over the place, and both of their rooms smelled like dirty socks and puke.

Sam and Willy roomed next to one another and never said a

word about their rooms. They just got up, ate, went to work, and usually came in late for supper. They were the best of friends, except sometimes after a card game when they wouldn't even talk to one another for as long as two whole days. That must have been hard, because they didn't have wives, any other friends, or even a dog. After those couple of days they'd be, as Uncle Ben would say, "asshole buddies" again until the next card game. Sometimes they woke me up yelling things like "You damned cheat" or "You dumb shit." I thought maybe if they played just for the fun of it instead of for money, they wouldn't have to get so mad so often.

Charlie roomed right across the hall, and he was really my favorite. He was the smartest person I ever knew except for Aunt Harriett, but he even knew things she didn't. He talked a lot about history and the United States. One day he told me we were going to lose our way. I didn't quite understand, 'cause I didn't know we were going anywhere. Then he began to talk about the day when the blacks would rise up against the whites, when all kinds of weird things between men and men, and women and women, would be going on right in public. He said he could see the day coming when our leaders would get so hungry with power that they would do only what they thought would serve them, never mind what would serve the rest of us. He said there would come a day when they felt so sure of themselves that they would "play nasty" with people they weren't even married to, and we would be too stupid to notice or so immoral ourselves that we wouldn't even care. He would most always end up talking about the Roman Empire—said we were going to suffer the same fate as the Roman Empire. A lot of what he talked about I really didn't understand, like that part about the Roman Empire. I think I knew what "play nasty" meant 'cause maybe that's what I heard Aunt Harriet and Uncle Ben doing some-times late at night when their bed would shake just like when the train went by. He read all the time and went every Saturday morn-ing to get some more books from the dump. I liked him so much that I really wanted to call him Uncle Charlie, but Aunt Harriett said that wouldn't be proper, so I never did.

His room was the most fun of all. Not only did he have piles of books everywhere, but he also had lots of other wonderful things that he got from the dump. There were pictures in frames—some of the frames a little cracked and some of the pictures a little moldy—but he said they were really worth saving. There were vases, a couple of sets of cups and saucers—and one set didn't even have a single chip in it—and some figurines. He had a nice rug on the floor that he told me was a Persian, whatever that meant, and an old tire standing in the corner. I don't know why he had the tire, 'cause he didn't even have a car, but I bet it was some kind of special one. As I said, his room was the most fun of all.

Sometimes when my aunt thought I was in my room coloring at my table, I would really be sneaking up and down the halls peeking in some of the other rooms. I usually didn't peek in Emma's room, because I was afraid she'd catch me. And I sure didn't bother to open the door to Willy's or Sam's, 'cause the smell would have knocked me over. But I had fun checking out the others until my aunt caught me. Then that was the end of that, so mostly I had to go back to hanging out in the kitchen.

The Survival of Mrs. Walden

Mrs. Walden was in charge of all the rooms—the whole house, in fact—and really tried to be in charge of seeing that we all got along really well. She was a short but sturdy person and kind of a pretty woman, or at least you could tell she used to be. She had dark hair and eyes and high cheekbones, and she always looked as though she'd been sunning herself. I heard Sam say one time after she had given him hell for peeing in the hallway that he knew something about her mother and Old Joe the Indian. I don't think she knew what he meant, 'cause she just turned and walked away. I wasn't sure what he meant, either. All I know is that she didn't speak to Sam for days after that.

Whenever she talked to me, she did it in a quiet sort of way, but mostly she talked loudly, as if she was shouting out orders, and she was always in a hurry, checking this, checking that. Aunt Harriet said she did that to keep the inmates from taking over the asylum, whatever that meant. The people in the house called her either Mrs. W or Wally, but I had to call her Mrs. Walden, not only because she was my elder, but out of respect for the great business-woman she was.

She hadn't always run a boardinghouse. In fact, when Mr. Walden was still alive, they just lived there—just the two of them in that big old place—but it was the house her husband bought when he came all the way up here from Philadelphia to die.

Aunt Harriet told me the whole story just as Mrs. Walden had told it to her and to no one else. It was kind of like a secret, a really sad one. The doctors had told Mr. Walden that he had only about two years to live, so he headed north looking for a quiet place to go out from. He picked our small town, 'cause it was as different from the city as you could get, and the big old house, 'cause it wasn't anything like the row house where he'd lived for years.

This place had needed a lot of work, such as fixing the big old wraparound porch and the leaky roof, so he found a young guy from town who had just quit working at the mill and hired him. When the guy came to work, he brought his younger sister to give him a hand carrying lumber and nails and stuff. And that's when old Mr. Walden first saw her. After just a couple of months, he went to her family and said he wanted to marry her.

They were a very large and very poor family, and because Mr. Walden had a lot of money and promised to take care of them all, they were as happy as pigs in shit. All except poor Mrs. Walden; she was only sixteen years old, and he was fifty.

"You'll do it," her father demanded. "No time to act like a goddamned princess or selfish son of a bitch. The old bastard will be dead in a couple of years, and we could all be better off. You've given us enough grief, you shitting half-breed; now it's time you thought about what we've done for you and do something for us for a change."

That's what Mrs. Walden told Aunt Harriet he had said, and she cried when she told her. She couldn't argue with her pa for fear of getting beaten, and all her mother did was sit in the corner and cry. My Aunt Harriet always told me we have choices in life, but I guess Mrs. Walden didn't have one that time. She married the old man, and he lived for seventeen more years.

At first things weren't too bad, once she got used to them and stopped crying herself to sleep. She had to work hard and do what he wanted her to, whenever he wanted her to do it. But he did some kind things also. He bought her some boots and a jacket for winter and even some shoes she could wear in the summer. She'd never had a pair of those before. Although she felt sad and lonely at times, she began to believe that it might be okay. Even if there was something about the arrangement that wasn't quite right—like no laughter, no friends, no time for fun—it still might be okay. He never complained when her family came by to borrow money or was looking for other handouts, so she began to believe she was meant to be there for their sake. At first it was okay, but only at first.

Things changed little by little, but five years later, on the very date they had been married, Mr. Walden threw her pa off that big old porch—took him by the seat of his pants and ditched him. He was swearing the whole time, and so was her pa. But old Mr. Walden had the last words when he shouted he never wanted to see his face or his ass around that place again. He even used the F word when he shouted those things, and it was downhill from there.

He turned real mean and began pushing Mrs. Walden around, telling her how useless she was and things like that. She could handle that part, even believed it was probably true, 'cause that's what her pa had always told her. But then he began acting really crazy, and it was the crazy part that scared her. Every day he'd go all through the house checking every room and peeking in all the closets. He was sure she had a boyfriend hidden somewhere. Sometimes he'd surprise her by jumping out from behind a door screaming, "Where is he, bitch, where is he?" It made her a wreck, but she never complained or told anyone. She tried to keep it hidden from the folks in town, but she couldn't hide it all.

At least twice a week he would send her to the small store down the street with a list of things they didn't even need—a can of this, two cans of that, three jars of whatever. Then he'd hide behind trees or in the back of houses along the way just to spy on her, to see if she talked to anyone, especially any men or boys. When she got home, he wouldn't let her unpack any of the bags. He would just order her to stack them here and there. Some went in the hallway, in the parlor, or all the way upstairs into the bedrooms. She told Aunt Harriet that she must have had more than a thousand bags of stuff all over the house before the old man finally died.

There weren't too many at his funeral. None of her family showed up. I guess they thought she'd let them down because the old bastard lived so long. A few townspeople came, some out of respect for Mrs. Walden, others out of curiosity. But not a one of them believed the minister when he talked about Mr. Walden as a kind man and loving husband. "Sure," they thought, "a loving husband who hides behind trees and spies on his wife." Those who knew her were pleased that she was now free and thought for sure she must be feeling some kind of relief. Now she could get on with a real life. But that's not exactly what she felt or what she did, at least not at first.

Back in that big empty house, she wrapped herself in an old Indian blanket, sat in a chair in the parlor, and rocked herself back and forth. Occasionally she'd cry or make moaning sounds, and that's how people who came to visit found her. After a few weeks people stopped dropping in. They just didn't know how to reach her. It was easier to let her be. They weren't really her friends, just folks who knew her and knew about her. For almost four months she was all alone, and all she did was rock and moan, rock and moan. The only time she left her chair was to wash her face, brush her teeth, go to the bathroom, or open a can of something to eat. She didn't bother to comb her hair or even go to bed to sleep. She had no idea why she reacted that way and guessed that God didn't, either. But one day out of the blue, it was over. She never spoke of the old man again, until the time she told Aunt Harriet the story.

The first thing she did was fold up that old Indian blanket and drag it up to the attic. Then, she said, she took a really long bath, cut off most of her hair, and began to put away all those damned groceries. It took her almost a week to sort out all the cans and jars, and she ended up storing most things out in the barn. She found a sign painter and had a sign made that read, Mrs. W's Place, and hung it on the front porch railing. Aunt Harriet said she really wanted a sign that read, Mrs. Walden's Boardinghouse, but because the painter charged by the letter, she settled for the shorter version. Be that as it may, she was open for business.

Sweet Aunt Harriet, Thrifty Uncle Ben

I think I was about three years old when Aunt Harriet, Uncle Ben, and I moved into the boardinghouse. Funny but I can't remember much of anything before the boardinghouse. I can't picture any other place or any other family from when I was a kid—just Mrs. W's Place and the people in it. For the most part, they were my family, and just like a real family, some of them I liked a lot and others I didn't like very much at all.

It wasn't until I went into the first grade that I began to wonder about a mother and a father. I guess that was because most kids had them. One time I heard that mine died right after I was born, but that was all, and it didn't seem quite right. Emma was the only one who ever mentioned it. Once in a while when no one else was around, she would grin and whisper to me, asking me if I wouldn't like to know who my mother really was. That sure stopped once I told my Aunt Harriet. Boy, did she get mad. She made me stay in my room when she went downstairs to have a talk with Emma. I'm not sure why it took so long when all she really did was tell Emma to mind her own damned business.

She got almost as mad the time Emma told me never to take a bath in the tub right after my brother 'cause that's how I'd get a baby. "Crazy old lady," Aunt Harriet shouted at her. "You leave any of those talks to me. I'm the one who will tell her what she needs to know. Stupid. . . . How could you be so stupid?" I thought it was pretty stupid myself 'cause I didn't even have a brother, at least not one I knew about.

Emma was the only one my aunt ever got mad at. Sometimes she'd shake her head when Kathy did something screwy, or she'd look kind of sad at Sadie and Shakespeare or cluck her tongue when Willie and Sam were extra drunk. But for the most part, she didn't get mad. I guess that was good, because when she did get mad, it sure wasn't pretty.

I thought my aunt was the most beautiful woman in the whole world until I went into second grade, and then my teacher took the top spot, but Aunt Harriet was still awfully pretty. She was quite tall, a little taller than Uncle Ben, had hair that was still a pretty red color, which must have pissed off Emma, and beautiful green eyes. In the summer she would get all kinds of freckles. She just hated them, but I wanted them so badly that I even tried to make me some with a little brown crayon. I wished I looked just like her, but all we had alike were the green eyes. In the summer I looked more like Mrs. Walden than I did my aunt.

Sometimes on a quiet afternoon, we'd cuddle up on her bed and she'd either read to me or make up stories. She'd talk to me about all kinds of things she thought I needed to know: about being fair to other people even when they weren't being fair to me, about always telling the truth, and things like that. She told me it did no good to complain about things around us. And when I asked her if she thought Emma would complain to God when she got to heaven, she just answered, "If she doesn't soon learn to be grateful for what she has, she isn't even going to get there." I knew right then that being grateful was something I should remember.

Once in a while she'd take a little snooze. Sometimes I did, too; other times I just lay there feeling pretty special because I had my aunt and the guardian angel watching over me. Before I was to start school, she gave me some ideas on how to act if the kids made fun of me because I lived at Mrs. W's instead of in a house of my own. She was really worried, but as smart as she was, I guess she didn't know a lot about other kids.

There were only twelve in my class, and it seemed nobody even knew where I lived, so one day I told them. Then I told them about what fun it was. Every day I had a different story. If I didn't have anything funny or crazy to tell them, I'd just make something up. Most of the time, what I made up was even better than the real stuff. By Christmas, half of them wished they lived at Mrs. W's, not only because it was so much fun, but because they thought all those people would probably be giving me lots of nice presents.

Aunt Harriet and Me

Uncle Ben was really the quiet one. Just like Aunt Harriet, he'd shake his head at some of the goings-on, but he hardly ever made any comments, and I never once heard him cluck his tongue. He was shorter than my aunt—a little thin man without much hair or very many wrinkles. His life seemed to be just as quiet as he was. He went to work in the mill every day, and even though he was some kind of boss, he worked right along with his men and most times worked even harder than they did. Sometimes when he was kind of sick, Aunt Harriet would tell him to stay home, but he never did. He'd just work, eat supper, and then go to the room to read the newspaper and listen to his radio. He used to laugh out loud at a show called "Amos and Andy" and be real quiet when he listened to "I Love a Mystery," and on Sundays he always listened to "The Shadow Knows" and "The Green Hornet." But that was it.

They were real nice to each other, and the only times I ever heard them fighting was when they talked about money. Most of the time she would tell me they weren't fighting, just talking loudly. But, boy, sometimes it got really, really loud. He didn't mind wearing worn-out clothes or shoes or a thin jacket in the winter. One time he even tried to line that jacket with newspaper to keep the wind from getting in. Boy, did that make Aunt Harriet mad. "You make good money, never spend a cent you don't have to. You don't drink, and you don't even play cards, so where the hell does your paycheck go? Buy a jacket for heaven's sake; go buy a jacket. You're making me ashamed."

She told me that time that it really was a fight, except he didn't fight back. He never said a word. The only time he ever gave Aunt Harriet a little extra money was at Christmas, and he gave me some also—three dollars as a matter of fact, which seemed like an awful lot coming from Uncle Ben. There were a couple of times when he did splurge. Once was when Kathy was in charge of supper because both Aunt Harriet and Mrs. Walden were feeling poorly. Mrs. Walden had told Kathy just what to do, but it was one of her not-listening times. Instead of following instructions, she decided to make a big pot of soup. She saw a pot that was filled with water simmering on the stove. I guess she didn't realize that Mrs. Walden had added a lot of baking soda so that all the burnt stuff on the bottom would let loose. She just threw in whatever leftovers she could find and let them simmer away. That soup was all we were to have for supper. Uncle Ben took one sip and then told Aunt Harriet and me to go to the room, turn on the radio, and wait, that he'd be right back.

He came in and showed us a small box of crackers, a small jar of peanut butter, and three cans of sardines. He said there was something special in the bag he was saving for last. We were going to have a picnic, right there in the room, with Amos and Andy. The sardines were terrible—big sardines packed in some kind of mustard sauce. Aunt Harriet said I should try to eat just a couple of them anyway 'cause Uncle Ben had been kind enough to buy them. Besides, he was so pleased that they were on sale. Three cans for fifty cents. I managed to gag down a couple, but knew I would never eat another sardine, ever, ever, ever! Then he pulled out the special treats: Whoopee Pies, two of them. One was for him and Aunt Harriet to share and the other just for me. I guess we didn't each get one of our own 'cause they weren't selling three for something, like the sardines.

My First Communion—I Learn to Confess and Go Christmas Shopping

There was another time Uncle Ben splurged: when it was time for me to make my First Communion. Mrs. Walden found some very pretty white material, and she and Aunt Harriet set out to make me a dress. Emma told me that what they were sewing was just some curtains that had been hanging around, but that didn't matter; I knew it would be beautiful. The Saturday afternoon they were putting on the finishing touches, Uncle Ben said he had an errand to run but wouldn't tell anyone, even Aunt Harriet, where he was going. When he came back a few hours later, he put a big bag on my bed. In it were some white stockings, a pair of white shoes they called Mary Janes, and a great white veil.

The veil was a little too big, "something a bride would wear," Emma said when she saw it, and the shoes a tiny bit too tight, but I had it all. I wouldn't say a thing about the shoes, and as far as the veil was concerned, I'd just pretend I was going to church to marry somebody, like the priest or Jesus or somebody. Aunt Harriet cried and cried, not because of the things Uncle Ben had bought, but just because he'd bought them. She must have said, "Thank you, oh, thank you, Ben," one thousand times.

Everyone went to church except Sadie and Shakespeare, even Willy and Sam. They never went before and never went again, not even on Christmas Eve. I was sorry Buster couldn't see how nice I looked, but he touched my nice long veil and then surprised me by running his fingers across my face. It was the first time Buster had ever touched anyone that I could remember. Then he quietly told me he could really tell that I looked beautiful.

Mrs. Walden fixed a great lunch with a big decorated cake and all. And at lunchtime Charlie even gave me a present: a pretty little statue of the Virgin Mary. Aunt Harriet grabbed it right away and decided to clean it up before she'd let me have it. She stuck it in some boiling water, and all the blue and gold paint peeled right off. All that was left was a little white thing, but I put it in my room anyway.

I was really excited about my First Communion but was scared to death about the confession part. I had the prayer down pat, the one that begins with "Bless me, Father, for I have sinned," but after the prayer, I wasn't so sure. Aunt Harriet kept telling me it wasn't anything to be afraid of; just go on in and tell the priest everything. I tried to listen, but, boy, when you're a kid and you're kneeling on a little wooden step in a dark closet and talking to a tiny screen with God's assistant on the other side, it can get scary, no matter what your aunt said.

The first time, I told the priest I swore a lot. When he asked if I had taken the Lord's name in vain, I told him no but I had said "shit" about 376 times. He told me that although that was not a very ladylike thing to say, it really didn't count. So I guessed I could say "shit" whenever I wanted as long as nobody at Mrs. Walden's heard me.

The second time I went, he kind of laughed when I confessed I had committed adultery. That really surprised me 'cause I didn't know that priests laughed. He asked me to explain just what I had done, so I told him I sometimes peed on the floor of the barn instead of going inside to the bathroom. I knew that wasn't right but didn't know which sin it fit under. He explained that I should always try to make it to the inside, because that would be the right thing to do, but that what I did wasn't adultery. He didn't go on to explain just what adultery was, so I never went on to explain how I sometimes had a hard time holding my pee.

The next few times, I figured I had the hang of it. I'd talk and talk, and he'd listen. After a while he'd simply say, "You know, my child, you are here to tell me your sins, not the sins of everyone else," but he was always kind enough to listen. That went on until the time Aunt Harriet was waiting her turn and got pretty upset because I'd taken so long. On the way home, I tried to explain because I didn't want her to think I had all those sins myself. She sure straightened me out, and I heard her mumble something about how she was also going to straighten out the "good Father," but, of course, she never did. Finally I figured out a real sin. I wanted all those nice things Charlie had in his room—except, of course, for the tire—and wanted them before Aunt Harriet had a chance to clean them up. I guessed that would fall under the "coveting" thing. It sure would have been easier if God had made only five or six simple commandments and then just made the rest of them as some suggestions. That would have been real nice, especially for kids.

The only other time most of us went to church together was on Christmas Eve. We would have a nice big Christmas dinner and then head out for church. It was only a short walk. Mrs. Walden would help Buster keep his footing, and Aunt Harriet would hold my hand all the way. She'd tell me to breathe in the bright, crisp air, listen to the crunching snow under our boots, and let the beautiful bells from church remind me of what Christmas was really all about. I tried to listen to every word, but it was kind of hard with Emma grumbling about how cold it was and how those darned bells were driving her crazy. Aunt Harriet was amazed that Emma never complained about how long the service took, but I guess that was because she sat up back and slept through most of it. The next morning we opened all our presents, and that was the best part of all.

The week before Christmas, Aunt Harriet would always take me on the morning train to the neighboring town to do our shopping. Most of the time we would come back on the train that left at four in the afternoon, except once when I peed my pants and refused to get on the train with wet bloomers. That time, Aunt Harriet hurried to buy me a new pair, but she still wasn't quite fast enough. We had to wait until seven o'clock that night before we could get home. She wasn't mad at me, though, probably because of the Christmas-spirit thing.

I always shopped in the same five-and-ten-cent store and usually bought the same things: little bottles of orange blossom perfume for the women and hankies for the men. I'm not sure the hankies were a good idea, because only Buster and Uncle Ben used them when they needed to, and Charlie used them only once in a while, I think so as not to hurt my feelings. Willy and Sam just used their shirtsleeves, except the one time Sam really blew his nose big and loud and into one of Mrs. Walden's napkins. She was really mad and called him a pig. "Yeah," he answered, "just wait till I use one of your precious napkins to wipe my arse. That'll teach ya." Boy, did he and Willy laugh, but nobody else did, especially Mrs. Walden.

It didn't take me too long to do my shopping, and I always managed to save enough money for an ice cream treat once Aunt Harriet had finished hers.

The Christmas after my First Communion, Uncle Ben bought me, all on his own, a little rosary. It was made out of pretty pink beads. He thought that if I had my own, I wouldn't have to use Aunt Harriet's big black pair. Maybe he also thought that if I had my own, I'd use them more often. I wasn't very good about that. That present made my aunt cry again.

That same year, Willy and Sam bought me a BB gun. Aunt Harriet made them take it back, real quick like, so they got me a cute little doll and a ball-and-jack set. Unfortunately it was the exact same thing Emma had bought me. I didn't mind, because I could pretend the dolls were sisters, and you're always losing the jacks anyway. But Emma had a hissy fit. She said they knew just what she'd gotten and got the same thing on purpose.

I got books from Charlie—I always got books—books that my aunt wouldn't let me handle myself, but she would thank Charlie and would always read them to me. Sadie and Shakespeare gave me a bag of Christmas candy again, and Buster gave me eight quarters all wrapped up. On my birthday he'd give me only four 'cause it wasn't as important as Christmas.

I was never sure what Kathy would give me; it was always a surprise. One year she gave me a knife, fork, and spoon that looked just like any I had ever seen, but she said they were very special because they were from her grandmother's solid-gold set of silver. I wasn't sure what a solid-gold set of silver was, but I used them every night at supper until she took them back.

One year I had a great idea for Emma. She just loved reading the newspaper and made sure she was the first one to get her hands on it. Nobody dared read the paper before Emma. She'd always read the bad things out loud to anyone who would listen, and then at supper she'd talk about them over and over again in case we'd missed something. She just loved news about fires, floods, earthquakes, bad accidents, and stuff like that. I thought that if I saved some of the bad pictures and pasted them in a little book and my aunt helped me draw some other ones that Emma could color, she'd really love it. When I told Aunt Harriet, she laughed and laughed—not at my idea, but because I'd thought of it. She then told me that we shouldn't help others dwell on bad or sad things, and we certainly shouldn't do that ourselves. It would only make us look at the world as a place where only bad things happen, and then, of course, we would feel afraid or sad most of the time. I guessed that was partly the problem with Emma, so I just bought her more perfume even though I never smelled her wearing it. Not like Kathy; I could smell that orange blossom stuff on her when she was as far away as the barn.

The Cook, the Baby, and the Hissy Fit

Suppertime at the house was when most things happened—funny things that I could tell my friends at school. Willy and Sam often made rude sounds when they were eating. Most times they were burps, but once in a while they'd make this sound and the smell would reach way across the table. Poor Mrs. Walden; I don't know how many times she told them that if they had to fart, go out in the hall, but they weren't ones for listening.

I got pretty good at describing different fart sounds. I could mimic loud ones, wet ones, ones that sort of trilled out, all kinds that I practiced on my way to school. My friends would really laugh, and on the playground they always wanted me to tell them fart stories and make fart sounds. One time we all decided to draw some pictures of farts, but that didn't work too well because none of us had ever seen one.

There were times at the boardinghouse when we ate supper at two different settings: in the winter when the men came to help harvest the ice and in the summer when the young guys from Tennessee came to help pick apples. Mrs. Walden had room for them to stay on bunks in the barn, but there just wasn't enough room at the table for all of us to eat together.

Having those extra people sure made a lot of work for Mrs. Walden, and even with Kathy and my aunt helping, there still seemed to be too much to do, so one time Mrs. Walden hired a cook named Mrs. Duquette to help out. Just one time, however.

Mrs. Duquette was an older lady, very plump. She wore housedresses that were way too long, heavy brown stockings, and old black shoes. Her hair was the only thing about her that looked really neat because she kept it pulled back in a big bun. She was really a good cook and knew how to serve, but she couldn't speak a word of English. I guess the problem started when Willy and Sam decided to give her lessons.

They told her potatoes were "turds," ham on the platter was called "pig's ass," butter was "slick shit," both coffee and tea were called "piss," and lots of other things. Perhaps it wouldn't have been so bad if Mrs. Duquette hadn't been a fast learner. She never listened to anyone else, just Willy and Sam, and when Mrs. Walden saw her big grin the day she asked if someone wanted more "turds," she suspected she knew more English than she had led anyone to believe. She also suspected that Mrs. Duquette had what she called "a thing for Willy," so she fired her. From then on, there never was any extra help, except for the short time Alice and her baby came to stay.

It was the first time we ever had a baby at the house, and I thought she was just the cutest baby in the world. The only problem was the boardinghouse didn't have any cribs or stuff like that stored out in the barn. Mrs. Walden, being the smart woman she was, simply took a drawer from Alice's bureau and put a pillow in the bottom so that the baby would have its own neat little bed. It didn't matter to Alice, 'cause she hardly had anything to put in her bureau anyway.

I would stand and watch that baby sleeping in her drawer for the longest time. All she really did mostly was sleep, but it was fun to watch anyway. I asked Aunt Harriet what Mrs. Walden would fix up for her to sleep in when she got too big for the drawer. She just told me not to worry; it would be a long time coming. For some reason, when my aunt looked at the baby, it seemed to make her a little sad. My Uncle Ben didn't even bother to ever look. I guess most men aren't interested in babies anyway.

Somebody was paying half the money for Alice to stay at the boardinghouse, and she was helping with chores to take care of the rest. Sometimes she was a little slow at catching on to what Mrs. Walden wanted her to do, but when she figured it out, she did really well.

Everyone liked Alice except Kathy. She didn't like her very much at all. Sometimes she'd call her names like Skunk, Miss-Know-It All, and Poop Head. Skunk was her favorite, though. I thought she was probably jealous because she didn't have a baby the way Alice did, but my aunt told me that wasn't it. She just said her nose was out of joint, but it looked the same to me.

Poor Mrs. Walden. Sometimes when she'd ask Kathy to do something, Kathy would just slam around and yell, "Let Skunk do it." For a few weeks she sure was a handful, but she never got fired. My aunt told me that was because she had no place else to go. She also told me just to stay out of her way when she was having one of her "hissy fits." That wasn't hard for me to do, because I remember what she did to that boyfriend she had one time.

His name was Fish Head. At least that's how he signed his name to the love letters he used to write and toss up on the porch. Sometimes in the afternoon he'd ride up on his bicycle and offer to take her for a ride. Sometimes she'd climb on, and sometimes not. But when she did go, he'd only peddle up one side of the street, turn around, and peddle back. I guess he got the idea from watching our town parades, because that's what they always did. The only difference was there were no people standing on the side of the street or sitting on their porches to cheer them going up and coming back.

One day she came stomping back, and poor Fish Head was pushing his bike alongside trying to talk to her. He was almost in tears, but she wouldn't listen; she just kept stomping and shouting things about him and about his mother. I couldn't really figure out what she was saying, especially the mother part, but she sure was mad. All afternoon Fish Head would peddle up and throw notes on the porch. She wouldn't even read them. She'd just tear them up and throw the pieces right back at him. That night he decided to try something different. He parked his bike under her window and began to sing something about a blue moon that saw him standing alone. I didn't hear the whole song, because he didn't know all the words. He just sang the first part over and over, trying his best to be romantic. Kathy finally opened her window, and I guess that because she didn't have any more notes to throw back at him, she just threw one of Mrs. Walden's flat irons instead. Aunt Harriet said it was really a good thing she missed him or he would have been dead for sure. That was the end of Fish Head; he didn't come around anymore.

After a few weeks she acted kinder to Alice, and they really became friends. In fact, they were such good friends that Alice would not only do her own chores, but do the ones Kathy was supposed to do whenever Kathy told her to. I guess that's why Kathy cried a few months later when Alice left the boardinghouse to go home to her own family.

Her family lived right there in town, way up on the old mountain road. I couldn't figure why she'd come to the boardinghouse in the first place if she had a family to go to. When I asked Aunt Harriet about it, she told me it was another one of those times when I should mind my own business, so I asked Emma instead.

Emma was delighted and said she'd tell me the whole story if I didn't tell Aunt Harriet that she told me. Emma was making it sound like a big exciting secret, something I shouldn't know and something that would make my aunt really mad if she ever found out she'd told me. So I crossed my heart and promised never to tell, and Emma began the story.

She said that when Alice went to the hospital to have her baby, the people there kept asking her who the father was. She kept telling them she didn't know. For a couple of days, they kept asking and she kept saying she didn't know. On the third day when they asked the same question, she answered, "I really don't know who the father is. It could be my pa or my brother." Then Emma told me she had heard from one of the nurses that Alice said she really hoped it was her brother because he was a better lover.

That's when the people at the hospital decided she shouldn't go home. They made arrangements with Mrs. Walden to take her in for half-price, and she could do some chores for the rest that was due. She'd had a birthday while she was with us and was now old enough to decide for herself where she wanted to live. She wanted to go home. Maybe she missed her folks, or maybe she was just sick of doing all of Kathy's chores.

Everyone seemed worried, and my aunt and Mrs. Walden had big, long talks with Alice late at night when no one else was around. Finally, when they knew she'd go home anyway, they decided to call the sheriff. All they did was ask the sheriff to go have a long talk with her brother and her pa. I guess one of those talks must have worked, because Alice didn't have any more babies as far as I knew.

A Room Sadly Empty, Summer Pickers, and Winter Icemen

Charlie surprised all of us the night we were having our Thanksgiving dinner. He told us he was going to head out west. He said he'd be gone only a few months and wanted Mrs. Walden to save his room. He bought an old van, picked up a stray dog, loaded up a few things, including his tire, and did exactly what he said he was going to do: He headed west. I thought it was really exciting because he was going out there to pan for gold.

It was weeks before anyone heard from him, and then finally we got a little postcard from somewhere in Arizona. He was doing just fine and gave us a post office box to use if we needed to get in touch with him in case there was an emergency. We didn't hear anything else all winter long, and then in April he came rolling in. He was still driving that old van and still had that old stray dog.

He very proudly presented me with a little glass jar that was filled with water and had little gold flecks that floated around when you shook it. That was the gold that Charlie had found—all of it, as a matter of fact—but he didn't seem to mind that he hadn't come back rich. He told me the experience had made him rich in other ways. We were all glad to have him back, and I was especially glad he hadn't been there when they took Sadie and Shakespeare away.

It had been a cold fall day when Sadie decided to hitch a ride all by herself to go for the candy. She was outside walking down the street with her thumb stuck out, bare-ass naked. My aunt and Mrs. Walden tried their best to drag her back inside, but she fought them like a tiger. Then Shakespeare got into the act and began fighting both of them. He was shouting for them to leave her alone. The only problem was he didn't have any clothes on, either.

There was such a ruckus that a neighbor called for help. The next thing you knew, they were both being loaded into some kind of state car, but at least now they were covered, Sadie in an old robe that belonged to my aunt and Shakespeare wrapped in a blanket. There was a lot of pleading and begging going on from the people at the boardinghouse. Even Emma was trying to persuade the state people to leave them alone. No matter what anyone said—and they had a lot of good things to say about Sadie and Shakespeare—the folks in the car weren't about to listen. They just kept saying they would take them someplace where they would be safe, someplace where they would be much better off.

That really started everyone screaming and yelling, everyone except Sadie and Shakespeare, who just sat quiet and sad like in the back seat. My aunt guessed that they must have had something like this happen to them before they'd found their way to Mrs. W's. Finally, when they all realized there wasn't anything they could do, my aunt packed up a few of their personal things and just threw them in the front seat of the car. The only thing she passed to the back was Mama. She was crying, and so was everyone else. They weren't crying, "Don't do this," anymore; they were just crying, "Please keep them together." Mrs. Walden told them she would pack up anything that was left, such as the big basket of Sadie's treasures and the cigar boxes, and store them in the barn for when they came back. But it didn't seem as though they were listening.

When Charlie heard the story, he just about went crazy. He was screaming about the damned government and power-hungry assholes who didn't know shit about what was best for anybody. That's why I was glad he wasn't there to see it all. He would have had such a fit that they might have taken him away right along with Sadie and Shakespeare.

Even though months had passed, Charlie did his best to find out where they were, but nobody would tell him anything. And that sure didn't make him happy. Each time he went out searching, he'd come back ranting and raving, and it would take hours for him to simmer down. Finally he stopped trying, partly because those people told him that if he didn't stop bugging them, they'd sic the sheriff on him, and partly because it was springtime, and that was the very best time for dump picking, so he had lots to do.

After a while everyone seemed to stop thinking about Sadie and Shakespeare—all except Mrs. Walden, I guess, because she left their room empty for the longest time and still kept their personal things in the barn. When the apple pickers moved in, she warned them all that those things were private property and that someday the folks who owned them would be back.

It was always fun to have extra people living in the barn. The apple pickers were the best, though. They came up from Tennessee in an old, rickety bus and were much younger than the men who stayed just a couple of weeks to help harvest the ice. The icemen were from towns all around us and always seemed just to want to go to bed after supper, but the apple pickers were real strangers from far away and couldn't wait to eat so that they could prowl around, meet some girls from town, and raise a little hell. Charlie said that if they had to work as hard as the men did who brought in the ice, they wouldn't be so full of piss and vinegar. I guess he was right, 'cause I watched the ice harvest just one time, and it sure didn't look like much fun.

Aunt Harriet told me it was a very important job and had to be done at just the right time or else nobody would have ice for the icebox come summertime. That's why they closed the mill, so that all the men who worked there could help, even Uncle Ben, and why the senior boys from high school were excused from all their classes. I stood with Aunt Harriet to watch the operation. I was already really cold because it had been a long walk to get to where the work was.

Along the way, I played all kinds of tricks on myself so as to make freezing to death feel like fun. I blew out my breath pretending it was smoke from some old cigarette. I tried to make believe I was a famous skater. Then Aunt Harriet told me to stop sliding my feet and walk right or else we'd never get there. That was okay because my skating wasn't working anyway; my toes were too stiff. I didn't want to pretend I was that little match girl in the Christmas story, 'cause I didn't want any angel to come to help, unless, of course, she could help me from having to pee. No matter what I tried, nothing much helped, but I sure wasn't about to complain.

I watched men way out on the lake with big saws cutting out blocks of ice. Then others with big, long poles guided those blocks down channels that had already been cut. They'd pass the blocks from one man to another trying to keep them from jamming up things until they got to the very end of the channel. Then there would be others who would guide the ice onto a big train track-looking thing that went way up to an opening in the top of the ice-house. That's when Uncle Ben came into the picture. I guessed he had the most important job of all. He sat in a truck and kept driving it back and forth, back and forth, and somehow that made the ice blocks travel up that track thing until they fell out of sight into the big old icehouse. I thought they had given Uncle Ben that job because he was the smartest man there, but Aunt Harriet said it was more likely they gave it to him because it was the warmest job they had. She was convinced they all knew about that damned newspaper inside his lousy jacket.

Everyone was real serious and working real fast and hard. No one seemed to be having very much fun except the boys. They were strutting around from job to job, doing whatever the older men told them to do, and laughing a lot. I guess they were just happy 'cause they didn't have to be in school. After a while I got real tired of watching the same thing over and over, so we headed for home. I don't think my aunt was tired of watching, but she sure did get tired trying to explain to me why the ice wouldn't melt. She explained over and over about the dark inside the icehouse and the sawdust that would cover the blocks, how that would keep them safe until we needed to buy some from the ice truck to keep our food from spoiling. No matter how many different ways she told me, I still didn't really know what she was talking about. But the one thing I did know for sure was I didn't want a job harvesting ice when I grew up, not even the one Uncle Ben had.

I never did get to see the apple pickers do their job. That probably would have been more fun 'cause it was in the summer-time, and almost anything is more fun in the summer. I wasn't upset because I couldn't go into the orchards, but Kathy sure was. Each time Mrs. Walden told her she couldn't go, she'd throw one of her hissy fits. Over and over Kathy would ask, and over and over Mrs. Walden would say no. Maybe if Kathy had asked to go in the daytime when all the pickers were there instead of after sup-per when she'd go with just one of them who promised to show her how it was done, she might have gotten permission. It was pretty hard for Mrs. Walden to hold her ground, because Kathy knew that some of the town girls were going to the orchard after supper and couldn't understand why she wasn't allowed.

"I'll tell you one more time, my young friend," Mrs. Walden shouted. "If those girls are out there after dark, those pickers are picking something other than apples." I wasn't too sure what she meant, but it must have been awfully good, because when the pickers left town, four of the town girls went with them. Two came back after a couple of weeks, but the other two went all the way to Tennessee. One of them was Alice, baby and all.

She came by to say goodbye and show us all how her little one had grown. I thought she'd gotten much bigger, but my aunt thought she wasn't nearly big enough, at least not for a one-year-old. And she also wasn't excited when Alice told her the baby could almost roll over without any help. I didn't know much about babies, so I thought that was pretty good, even when no one else did. Everyone worried about Alice and the baby on that bus going so far from home, but my aunt and Mrs. Walden agreed that she might be better off in Tennessee than on that mountain with her brother and pa. Even though they didn't quite believe her when she said she was going to get married, they still guessed she'd never be back.

After they left, it took Kathy about three weeks to simmer down. She'd walk around mumbling about Tennessee just as though she'd lost the chance of a lifetime. And when she was in one of those moods of hers, she'd lash out at everybody and say things that didn't make any sense. She even got mean, calling Buster a mole and Charlie a dirty old dump man. She said Uncle Ben's new haircut made him look like a porcupine. She lashed out at Willy when he talked about liking salt in his beer. She said he was a dumb ass if he put salt in his beer. She said she had an uncle who did that and he died. When Willy asked how that happened, she answered, "He got hit by a train; what did ya think?" just as if that proved what a dumb ass Willy really was because he couldn't figure it out for himself.

Every night at supper she'd come up with something crazy, but nobody laughed. We all knew that laughing would only make her act out more, so we just waited it out. Finally she got back to being her old self. It wasn't that she was suddenly all okay, but only the way she used to be before the pickers came. It was a hard time for Mrs. Walden, and she vowed that next summer when that bus came rolling into town, those guys were going sleep in it. She wasn't about to rent them space in her barn ever again. Uncle Ben said she'd probably change her mind if she really needed the money.

A Shock for the Good Old Sports

There was a group in town of really important people who called themselves the Good Old Sports. They rented the grange hall every New Year's Eve, and that's where almost everyone, even some kids, went to celebrate. Once, Mrs. Walden gave in and let Kathy go, but then she told her never again. And once, Willy and Sam went, but the Good Old Sports were the ones who told the two of them never again. New Year's Eve was a big deal but not nearly as big as the weeklong winter carnival they put together year after year.

It always started with a parade that went the usual route: up one side of the street and back down the other. They held ski races on the very small mountain that was right across from the boarding-house. I thought it was more fun watching people get all caught up in the rope tow trying to get to the top than it was watching them ski back down. They had figure-skating contests, even though not many knew how to figure-skate. Mostly they just skated backward a lot or skated with one foot up in the air. Once in a while someone would twirl around, or at least try to. I could watch all the skaters from my aunt's bedroom window. It was like having a front-row seat.

I didn't bother to pay much attention to the ice fishing. Even though I knew the fisherman who caught the biggest fish would get a great big prize, there really wasn't much to watch. One year they didn't even have to measure the fish because only one guy caught one. There were also a couple of years when nobody caught anything, so they just saved the prize for the next year's carnival. They weren't about to give away anything for trying. They just said, "Try is try, but do is do."

The biggest event of all was the carnival ball to end all the weeklong fun and games. They decorated the big old grange hall with all kinds of streamers, cardboard snowmen, snowflakes, and other stuff. One year they even had hundreds of crepe-paper roses. Aunt Harriet said those roses didn't have much to do with a winter carnival, but someone in town had just learned how to make them, so they used every single one of them.

I didn't get to see the actual ball, but the day before, my aunt would walk me down so that I could see how pretty the hall looked. Everyone said the greatest excitement of all was when they stopped dancing right in the middle of the ball so that they could crown the winter carnival queen. The queen's prizes were sure greater than the stupid one they kept holding for the fisherman. There was always a hope chest—cedar lined no less—filled with all kinds of gifts people gave. There were home-knitted sweaters, socks, mittens, and hats. There were boxes of writing paper, candy, perfume, lipstick, and a pair of boots that could be exchanged for the right size in case they didn't fit. There were all kinds of good things but really no surprises. Most years the prizes were the same 'cause it was the same people who gave them.

Charlie was just standing on the sidelines the night they announced I was voted that year's carnival queen. He laughed and laughed. He laughed at those very important Good Old Sports, who were in a state of shock and weren't sure what to do next. He laughed at the mothers of the girls who were really hoping for this great honor and were really pissed off when they didn't get it. He said it served them right for the way they ran the contest.

It wasn't run like most contests where people voted for the brightest or prettiest girl in town. The Good Old Sports sold tickets, and for a dollar you could write in any name you wanted. There were six high school girls in the running, and their mothers sold a lot of tickets but not nearly as many as Willy and Sam had. Those two had gotten boxes of tickets and gone to every beer joint they had ever been in, and some new ones they discovered while on their mission. They sold tickets to their old drinking buddies and to some new ones. They left tickets with the bartenders, who told everyone to write in my name. I got more votes than anyone ever had in the entire winter carnival history, and I was only ten years old.

The president of the Good Old Sports paid a call on Aunt Harriet to see if they couldn't reach some kind of agreement since the whole town seemed upset. First she simply told them to go with the girl who came in second. That would be fine with her, but it sure wasn't fine with Willy, Sam, Charlie, or Uncle Ben. Willy and Sam complained because they'd worked so hard. Charlie said that it was a good lesson for those damned fools and that now maybe they would change the way they did business. He never thought it was fair anyway. Charlie was always one for fairness. And Uncle Ben thought that the hope chest had real value and that I should at least get that.

They gave me the hope chest, but I had to put it in the parlor because it was too big for my room. At first when Emma looked at it, she mumbled, "Well, this belongs to a queen who they should have crowned with a beer bottle!" She said that until one day when Aunt Harriet heard her, and then she didn't say it anymore. They let me keep the cardboard crown all decorated with sparkly things, because Willy and Sam insisted. But they kept the rest of the stuff for next year's queen except for the candy. I guess they figured it would get all wormy before winter rolled around again.

They decided not to send my picture to any newspapers the way they had of other queens in the past. That was probably a good thing, because people in town were already mad enough. They were mostly mad at Willie and Sam, but some, especially the mothers, were also mad at me when winning wasn't even my fault. That really ticked Charlie off, but he decided something good came out of it after all. He was damned sure that they would be running their stupid contest in a little different way come next year.

My Friends Della
and Little Mary Theresa

I didn't have kids come and sleep over, even though a lot of friends wanted to. Aunt Harriet didn't think it was too good an idea, but then neither did I. Emma would probably act the way she always did, but she sure wasn't any fun. They could peek at Charlie's stuff if he were around to show them. But if Buster didn't bump into something coming to the table, if Willy and Sam weren't kind of drunk and farting at the table, or Kathy didn't have one of her hissy fits or do something crazy, then they might think the stories I told them were all just made up. I did get to go for sleepovers, mostly to my best friend Little Mary Theresa's house, and once I even got to go to Della's house.

Uncle Ben wasn't happy about Della being my friend. He worked at the mill with Della's "old man" and told Aunt Harriet that he wasn't sure my going to their house was a good idea. After that he didn't say any more. He let my aunt make the final decision just as he always did, so I got to go.

The family, all ten of them, came to get me in their big old truck on a Saturday afternoon. When my aunt saw that, she sure had second thoughts, but she just told me not to sit on the homemade benches in the back of the truck; just sit on the floor and hang on—we didn't have far to go. It was a good thing she didn't know that we weren't going right to the house but all the way to the neighboring town so that Della's mother could grocery-shop in the big store.

Della, her three sisters, and I went to the grocery store with her ma. The boys just spread out in different directions, and her old man went for a beer. I couldn't believe the baskets full of groceries. There seemed to be tons of stuff, even more than Mrs. Walden bought for the house. It took us a whole hour before we finished up and got back to the truck.

There they were, the old man and all the boys, huddled around the back of the truck just looking at piles of stuff. Della told me that whoever had been able to steal the most was going to get a fifty-cent reward. There was a flashlight, a couple of belts, three packages of socks, a hammer, bags of candy, some shampoo, and lots of other stuff. But the brother who had stolen twenty-four tooth-brushes got the prize. It was a game they played every Saturday night, and Della and her sisters didn't think much about it one way or another, but I sure did. I thought about it all the way to their house, but once inside when we started playing games and chasing the chickens around, I didn't think about it again until we went to bed.

Della's house was sure different from Mrs. W's. It had only one floor, which I thought was good 'cause there would be no place for ghosts to hide. The kitchen was really big. It seemed much bigger than the one at the boardinghouse, maybe because it didn't have so much stuff in it. There was only a big old wood stove, a long table with lots of chairs, and a big old sink without running water. The boys were the ones who were supposed to bring in pails of water from the well, but when I was there, I noticed the girls mostly did it.

On one side of the kitchen was their parlor. They had a piano in one corner, a big old raggedy-looking sofa, and a bed for Della's ma and pa. Nobody used the parlor much unless they were gathered around the piano for a sing-along. Della told me they did that usually when her pa wasn't around.

On the other side of the kitchen was a shed that led to the barn. It had shelves for all the groceries, a cooler to keep things cold—even the milk they got from the cows—and a wooden thing with paddles in it so that they could make their own butter. The toilet was a three-holer way in the back of the barn. I didn't know if three people went to the toilet at the same time and didn't think it would be polite to ask. But I knew for sure I didn't want to walk through that big old barn to pee, not unless Della and all her sisters went with me.

Along the back side of the house were the two big bedrooms, one for the girls and one for the boys. There were no bureaus, just planks on bricks that were used for shelves, and each room had a big old closet. There weren't any windows in either of the rooms, so nobody had to worry about hanging curtains, and if you didn't have curtains, I guess you didn't have to worry about matching bedspreads, either. Each room had a big old bed and looked the same, except the boys had a cot in theirs for the oldest brother to sleep on. Della told me that someday soon her pa was going to get a cot for the girls' room, as well.

When I slept over at Mary Theresa's, there were two of us in one bed, and even there I had trouble not having a bed, even a little one, all to myself. At Della's, there were five of us—three sleeping with their heads up at the top, the other two heads down. I got to sleep up because I was company. I'm not sure if it was thinking about the stealing again, having to go out barn to pee, or those feet and legs coming up at me that kept me awake, but I sure didn't sleep very well.

The next morning they took me to church just as they promised my aunt they would. When all the Latin sing-song stuff wasn't putting me to sleep, I was thinking about the stealing. I wondered if I should tell the priest about that Saturday-night contest the next time I went to confession. But then I remembered getting into big trouble with my aunt for telling him about everybody else's sins and not my own, so I just told her instead. The only other time I ever got to go back to Della's was for her birthday party. I think my aunt felt a little sorry for Della because not many kids were going.

It was an okay party. At first we had fun chasing the chickens around the house, and then we went outside and had a cow-flap fight. But before we got to eat the birthday cake, we had to eat lunch. We each got a big plate of fish hash. It was even worse than those old sardines Uncle Ben had bought, but I ate it anyway. When I got home I had to have a bath and change clothes because I had cow manure all over me. After that I never got to go back for anything.

Mary Theresa was really my best friend. Most people called her Little Mary Theresa because her mother's name was also Mary Theresa. Some people called her mother Old Mary Theresa. I guess it was the only way they could tell them apart. Aunt Harriet and Uncle Ben were always very happy when I got invited to her house, because her family was about as religious as you could get.

Her mother would never miss church. She led the choir, and

even though those five people couldn't sing very well, she never gave up trying to teach them how. She was the one who put flowers on the altar on Sundays and was in charge of the Saturday-night bean suppers. She made Mary Theresa's three brothers be altar boys, even though they really didn't want to be. And if during the service they made faces or fooled around on the altar, they had to stay after church and say a whole bunch of extra prayers. Those three were always saying extra prayers. It wasn't because they committed sins or anything like that, but just because they were always doing something that drove their mother crazy.

Little Mary Theresa didn't have to say extra prayers very often, and the only thing she had to do at church was help dish out the beans. I think she really liked doing that; it made her feel very important, probably because her mother made sure she was at the head of the line so that everyone could see her serving.

Whenever I stayed over with Mary Theresa, we made darn sure we checked out her bed before we climbed in. One time her brothers put several frogs between her sheets. Boy, did we scream. We jumped around and screamed and screamed. The boys had to come and collect them all and then do their penance. That's what her mother called all those extra prayers: "doing your penance." I wasn't too sure exactly what that meant, and I wasn't too sure all those extra prayers helped at all. Maybe they would have helped Della's brothers, but they didn't do much for Little Mary Theresa. That night when they had finished praying, they just came into our room making all sorts of hissing sounds and telling us that next time it would be snakes, just as soon as they could find some.

They were always telling us horrible stories to try to scare us. They'd tell us about one-legged men and about great big guys with bulging eyes and long, greasy hair and hooks for hands that smelled like outhouses. They made up stories about bats that got all tangled up in girls' hair, about vampires, ghosts, and the werewolves that lived in the woods right behind their house. One time they even told us that Old Joe the Indian was roaming around town looking for young girls.

Old Joe lived with his only daughter in a shack in the woods. I had seen him only once, and he looked okay to me, the way I thought an old Indian should look. And I never heard that he did anything bad to anybody—unless, of course, it was to Mrs. Walden's mother awhile back.

We didn't believe most of the stories, but Little Mary Theresa did worry some about the werewolves, and I worried some about ghosts—mostly because of old Mr. Walden roaming around the attic. Sometimes when I was walking down the hall at the boardinghouse, a door would open and then slam shut, and nobody would be there. So I knew for sure there were such things as ghosts.

Even though we knew they were making up all that stuff, it was still hard to get to sleep, especially when they hid outside our door and made weird noises. They would moan and groan, rattle the doorknob, and scratch on the door.

"Oh, it's only the boys," we'd tell each other. Then the next minute we'd ask, "But what if it isn't?" Once when they kept at it for a really long time and we couldn't get to sleep, I thought Little Mary Theresa should go tell her mother. No way was she going to do that, because you got extra prayers just for being a tattletale.

One night we all got to "do penance," and it wasn't much fun. Instead of hiding outside the door, the boys decided to come barging in. One of them stepped right into Little Mary Theresa's chamber pot and tipped the whole thing over. We all had to take turns mopping up the pee and washing down the floor, and then we were marched down to the kitchen, where her mother had put some dry beans in all the corners. That's where we had to kneel on our bare knees. Her mother passed out the rosary beads and told us to begin praying out loud. I always thought saying the rosary took a little too long. Even with the pretty beads Uncle Ben gave me, there just seemed to be too many prayers to say in one sitting. That night it felt as though I had to say more than a trillion Hail Marys. If I hadn't been kneeling in the same corner as Little Mary Theresa, I might not have gotten through it. Both of us tried hard not to cry, and the boys were trying hard not to laugh. Although I didn't say anything to my friend, I couldn't for the life of me figure out what the Blessed Virgin had to do with a dirty old chamber pot and spilled pee.

Most of the time, at least when it was daylight, we could forget about the stories the boys made up, although I will say that when we were outside, we did stay away from the woods where the werewolves were supposed to live. But the stories that Old Mary Theresa told us weren't so easy to forget, because she was a grown-up and swore they were true. My friend and I used to talk about those stories, sometimes over and over. They were usually about kids our age who had been punished by God because they did something they shouldn't. Her God was always watching us and, boy, could he hand down some really bad punishments.

She told us about the kid who was always telling lies until one day when he got real sick, and then after that he could hardly talk at all, even when he wanted to tell the truth. She told us about a girl who was so disrespectful in church that she'd sit there Sunday after Sunday chewing big wads of gum and not paying any attention to her prayers. That one got me really thinking, especially after she said something made the girl swallow one of her big wads, and she had to have an operation because all that gum made a big ball that got stuck in her stomach. She told us story after story. She even cried a little when she told us about the kids who went for a joy ride instead of going to church and all got killed when the car they were riding in got hit by a train. That was supposed to have happened right here in town, but even Emma couldn't remember it when I first told her. And believe me; that was just the kind of thing Emma sure would have remembered.

My aunt also used to tell me stories about God, but they were always about a loving God, not a "Ha, I got ya!" kind of God. It got me a little mixed up in my thinking. If there were only one God, then I really wanted to believe he was the one who watched over us, gave us guidance and protection, and surrounded us with his light and love, just as my aunt said, and not a God who watched every move we made just so that he could punish us. Even though I really believed my aunt more than I did Old Mary Theresa, I still decided I wasn't going to take any chances. I wasn't even going to chew gum in church anymore.

I never told my aunt about Old Mary Theresa's stories, because I was afraid she wouldn't let me stay there anymore, and it was the most fun place in town, even with getting scared and everything. I did tell the stories to Emma, because they were just the kind of things she loved. She made me tell the one about the kids in the car three or four times until she finally decided she probably did remember it and it was just an awful, awful day with bodies all over the tracks and screaming parents and other gruesome stuff. Then she began to tell me the same story back again, and each time it got worse and worse until I wouldn't listen anymore. But when she said she would tell me about Old Mary Theresa, I decided to listen real good.

Emma said that right after Old Mary Theresa graduated from high school, she decided she wanted to be a nun. She found out just where she had to go and what she had to do. She told everyone in town that she was going to dedicate her life to serving the Lord, and everyone was so pleased that they made one of the Saturday-night bean suppers into a kind of going-away party for her. She had her bags all packed, even though she had to wait two weeks before it was time to leave. That's when Robert showed up.

Robert knocked on her door selling Raleigh products. Her family didn't buy anything, but Robert kept coming back, three times in one week. The second week when he showed up, Old Mary Theresa just grabbed her packed bags and ran off with him to get married. They didn't come back to town for a couple of years, probably because she figured it would take that long for the folks in town to forget about that nice going-away party.

At first they moved in with Old Mary Theresa's parents, who were as pleased as punch to have her back. They not only really liked Robert; they acted as though he'd somehow rescued their daughter. They told her over and over that being married to Robert and being a good wife was just as good as being married to the Lord. It took them three years to build their own little house, but they built it as fast as they could because with Old Mary Theresa having babies right in a row, her parents' house was just too small. There wasn't room for her and all those babies.

They settled into their own little place, and for the next five years they seemed to be a perfect family. Robert never missed a day's work, and Old Mary Theresa kept the house and the kids spotless. Of course, they never missed Sunday Mass or the Saturday-night suppers, and when they came into the church or the basement, everyone would marvel at the three boys and sweet little girl they were tugging along. Then something terrible happened. This is the part of the story that excited Emma the most.

One cold winter morning, Robert decided he'd go across town to start the stove for an elderly lady who lived all alone. Robert was like that, always doing things for others. According to Emma, Old Mary Theresa begged him not to go. Over and over she begged him, but he went anyway, and the whole house blew up.

At the wake and funeral she told everyone that this was God's punishment for not living up to her promise to become a nun. Neither Emma nor I believed it. She was a good wife and good mother, and why would God punish her and her four little kids? But I guess it doesn't matter what Emma or I believed; the sad part was that Old Mary Theresa believed it.

Messed-Up Willy and Poor, Stubborn Bastard Zeke

Maybe there are times when God really doesn't watch over us, when he lets things happen that aren't very fun, just to get a message across. Like the time with Willy.

Willy complained for two days about a horrible toothache, but he didn't want to take the time, spend the money, or go all the way to the big town to find a dentist. So one night when he was really extra drunk, he went into the barn and got himself a pair of pliers. He sat on that big old porch and pulled and pulled and pulled, and Sam just sat there and watched. Willy pulled out four of his teeth before he got what he thought was the right one. Come to find out he hadn't come anywhere close.

Mrs. Walden said the porch was a mess, but that's all she said. She just went about washing off the blood and sweeping away those old teeth. I didn't have a chance to see the porch, but I sure did see Willy, and he had to be a bigger mess than that old porch was. Boy, was he mess! It was days before he could eat or speak right, and Sam, even though he still had all his teeth, stayed real quiet and acted as though he'd lost his appetite. My aunt told me Sam was probably having "sympathy pains," something I didn't quite understand. But I thought I understood why God let all that happen. It was because he wanted Willy and Sam to get the message that they shouldn't get so "shit faced" so often. It was a nice try on God's part, but as near as I could tell, the message lasted only a week or two.

Charlie had a friend named Zeke. He lived on the opposite side of the mountain from Alice and her family, and every once in a while Charlie paid his friend a visit, but he always came back with the report that things were just the same, nothing new.

When Zeke's brother Ephraim came to town for a few supplies, everyone asked about how his brother was doing, and he always answered, "Rugged, rugged as a bear," until one day when he answered, "Dead, dead as a doornail, the poor bastard." Most people felt kind of bad, but none felt as bad as Charlie, and it was Charlie who told me the whole story.

When Zeke was just a young man, he fell madly in love with a girl from out of town. She had come for a brief visit with relatives and then stayed for the whole summer. She might have gone home after a couple of weeks if hadn't been for Zeke, but she ended up being just as crazy about him as he was about her. Her name was Shelia.

Shelia lived more than one hundred miles away, but that sure didn't stop Zeke. At least twice a week he'd hitch rides so that he could see his girl. He even hitchhiked all winter long. When summer came and he told his folks he was going to marry Shelia, all hell broke loose.

They hadn't fought him when he was doing all that traveling back and forth, 'cause I guess they were pretty sure he'd soon get sick of it. But Zeke hadn't tired of it at all; he was too much in love. After all, his brother Ephraim had lots of girls, fell in and out of love over and over again. They didn't understand that Zeke was not Ephraim, nor did they have any idea of just how stubborn a young man he really was. But they learned once they put their foot down.

Nobody quite understood why his parents objected to Shelia, but they sure did, and there was no way in hell they were going to let those two get married. Charlie said they fought night and day, and he never understood why Zeke hadn't just taken off and left home, but he hadn't. He just took to his bed instead and swore he'd never get up.

At first they'd drag him out of bed and give him a damned good beating, but when it was over, he'd crawl right back in. Over and over again he'd take the beatings but wouldn't give in. He was bound and determined that they let him marry the love of his life, and they were just as determined it wouldn't happen. Finally, after months of nobody budging an inch, his pa just said, "Let the stubborn bastard lie there." And that's exactly what Zeke did, for forty years.

Charlie said that after a while, Zeke couldn't have gotten up even if he wanted to. His family didn't beat him anymore, just took care of him as if he were a baby. He never had a haircut or a shave, and his fingernails grew so long and hard that they just curved around and around. Charlie told me that the last time he'd visited, all he could think of was that Zeke looked more like some kind of animal rather than a man, but he knew that the real Zeke was inside that pathetic body somewhere. Now he was dead—"dead as a door-nail, the poor bastard."

I wanted to learn more, like how did his ma and pa feel now, and what happened to Shelia? Charlie said he didn't give a damn about how the ma and pa were feeling. After all, it was from them that Zeke got his goddamned stubborn streak, and nobody knew anything about Shelia after all these years. Besides, he told me it made him both mad and sad, so he didn't want to talk about it any-more. He was just going to the dump to do some picking and get his mind off the whole sorry mess.

I wished I knew what happened to Shelia, and I wished Charlie had taken me on one of his visits so that I could have seen Zeke for myself. The only one who wished she had seen him more than I had was Emma. I never did learn any more, but I know the story Charlie told me was the God's honest truth, not only because other people in town told the same story, but because Charlie would never, ever lie to me.

Just an Indian

The trains went by about eight times a day. The passenger trains always stopped, but all the freight trains did was slow down. They slowed down enough so that the tramps could jump right off. I don't think they really went slow to give the tramps a chance, but that's how it worked anyway, and the first place they came to was the boardinghouse.

They came right up to the back door, knocked loudly, and asked Mrs. Walden for a handout. She always had something for them, like a big slab of homemade bread with butter and something left over from the night before. She'd just pass it out to them, and then they'd go away, but not before they made a little mark on the door to let other tramps know it was a good place to stop. Uncle Ben used to worry about those tramps, and over and over he told Mrs. Walden she should be careful. Since Uncle Ben wasn't one to be saying much, she probably should have listened.

One day after she cut the piece of bread, she put the knife on the old kitchen table and went to the refrigerator to get some leftovers. When she turned around, there was the tramp right inside the kitchen holding that big old bread knife. Was she ever scared, but not as scared as the tramp was when she started to scream. She screamed so loudly that he just took off a running, didn't even stop long enough to pick up his bread or put down the knife. That sure made everyone in the house a little nervous. It also made Mrs. Walden decide not to feed the tramps anymore, no matter how harmless they looked, so she made a sign with all the words she wanted because she wasn't paying anybody to print it for her. She just put up this big old board that said in big black letters, DON'T BOTHER TO KNOCK BECAUSE THERE AIN'T NO FOOD

HERE FOR YOU OR ANYBODY ELSE!!!

It was only a couple of weeks later when they found the body of Old Joe the Indian's daughter lying on the railroad tracks. At first the sheriff said her throat had been cut and her body just dumped on the tracks. Later he changed his mind and said a train had simply hit her, so there was no need to do anything else except bury her. Almost everyone in town believed the train story, but not everyone. Old Joe the Indian didn't believe a word of it, and neither did Charlie.

Charlie stomped around the boardinghouse for days just ranting and raving. He even found the sheriff and told us he'd given him an earful, "really told the idiot a thing or two." But it didn't change a thing. "By God," he said, "this just ain't fair. If this was anybody else's daughter, not Old Joe's, they would have busted their ass to get to the bottom of it." He tried to get others to listen to what he was saying, but not too many did. I guess they thought it didn't matter all that much since she was just an Indian.

My Aunt's Friends Josie and Becky

My aunt had some women friends in town she would visit every once in a while, or they would come to visit her. There were two who seemed like her favorites. I think she paid more attention to those two because they really did need a kind person to be their friend.

One was a tall, lanky, skinny old farmer named Josie. The other, Rebecca, was a tiny, polite, pretty little lady who folks said came from blue blood, whatever that meant. They are now both dead, and even if they died in different ways, they are still dead— dead as doornails, just like that poor bastard Zeke.

Josie always wore overalls and men's black shoes. I can't really tell you what color her eyes were, 'cause her glasses were so thick you could hardly see them, and she couldn't see a thing without them—not blind like Buster, but just about. She had grubby-looking hands and big feet, and if it weren't for her long, stringy brown hair, you might have thought her to be a man. She talked the way some men do with a deep, gravelly voice and could swear as good as Charlie, Willy, or even Sam. Josie mostly came to the house; in fact, I don't ever remember my aunt walking up to the farm to visit her. It was a good distance away, and I guess visitors weren't really welcome.

It was a big farm with vegetable gardens, blueberry patches, a cornfield, Christmas trees, a bunch of chickens, and even some pigs. Josie had to tend to it all, so I guess that was a big part of her problem. She had to plant everything and keep out the weeds, and when things were right for picking, she had to do that, too. She'd pick all the vegetables that were good and ready, load them in a wagon, and head off to sell them to the big store in the next town over. She did the same thing with the blueberries and Christmas trees. I thought that if she sold her stuff right here in town, it would be a lot easier, but my aunt told me that wouldn't work. She had to get a good price for everything and sell it all at once. It especially wouldn't work with the blueberries and Christmas trees, because people in town knew just where on the mountain they could pick their own berries and where in the woods they could find their own trees to chop down. All she ever sold in town were the eggs from that bunch of chickens. She'd come into town twice a week with a whole load and go door to door. That's when she'd stop by to visit my aunt.

Every time she came, she always had sad stories to tell and new bruises to show Aunt Harriet. The time I remember the most was when she came with only one side of her thick glasses still good. Her old man had really smacked her hard—so hard he'd knocked her to the ground—and when she managed to get up, part of her glasses was busted. She sure was crying about how hard it was to get her work done when she could hardly tell the plants in the garden from the damned weeds. It took her two weeks before she could get a new pair, and when Aunt Harriet told her how nice they looked, I knew she was fibbing, 'cause they looked just like the old ones and not nice at all.

My aunt would tell her over and over that she should leave, just take her little girl and get the hell out. But Josie had no place to go and no way to make a living if she wasn't out there farming. At least that's what she'd answer my aunt. If she had followed my aunt's advice, things might have turned out better.

We'd had a real hot dry spell, and Josie was doing everything she could to keep the gardens alive and the pigs and chickens happy. She was pretty tired and really worried about how things would turn out when her old man began to threaten her. He said either she'd make sure they got a good crop to sell or he would beat the living shit out of her. He told her this time he'd really bust her glasses and see that she didn't have one red cent to buy another pair. Aunt Harriet said she thought poor Josie must have just snapped. She went into the barn and got the shotgun, and as her old man was driving out in the wagon to go for a beer or two, she shot. She missed him, but a bullet bounced off the wagon and hit him in the cheek. He wasn't going to die or anything, but poor old Josie was sure in a lot of trouble. They were going to try her for attempted murder.

Every single day for the next three weeks while she waited for the hearing, she came by the boardinghouse. She and my aunt would sit at the old card table in the corner of the parlor. She would cry and cry, so afraid she would have to go to jail for the rest of her life, and my aunt would talk and talk, trying to convince her it would never happen. Everyone knew how abusive her old man was; half the town wished she hadn't missed, and the other half wished they could have shot him themselves. But nothing my aunt said seemed to make any difference, and it got to the point where she just couldn't take it anymore. Both Uncle Ben and Mrs. Walden told her she should quit trying, 'cause it was just plum wearing her out. So two days before the hearing when Josie came around, my aunt didn't even come downstairs. She just waited in her room until Josie left. From her bedroom window she watched Josie walk up the tracks with her head down, her shoulders stooped, and those big old shoes just plodding along. She walked way up out of town until she came to the bridge, and that's where they found her shoes and her glasses. Everyone in town knew then that Josie wouldn't have to worry about any old hearing.

Poor Aunt Harriet. For three days she just sort of wandered around the boardinghouse crying a lot and mumbling that maybe she should have talked to Josie that last morning as she had so many times before. No matter what Uncle Ben or Mrs. Walden said about how hard she had tried and how much she had given, their words didn't mean much. But when Josie's old man came storming in demanding the pig money, she stopped her crying and just decided that Josie was really in a better place after all—a place where that mean old bastard could never get to her again, ever again.

Nobody could figure out why it had taken the old man three whole days to figure out that there weren't any pigs to slop. Josie had sold them all, and that sure pissed him off, especially since he couldn't find the money. He was more upset about that pig money than he was about Josie jumping off that bridge in the first place.

He kept coming around. He was just dead sure that my aunt had all that money, but, of course, she didn't. Mrs. Walden told him to stay away, but that didn't work for a minute. It took Willy, Sam, and Charlie to throw him off the place before he took the hint.

My aunt finally found out where the two thousand dollars in pig money was. Josie had given it to a neighbor who used to tend to her little girl when things got rough around the farm. It was just a small amount of money, but she wanted to make sure there was something for her daughter. My aunt never told, and when the old man left town ranting and raving about that pig money, everyone in town was happy to see him go. They were even happier when the neighbor was given Josie's little girl to raise. My aunt told me that Josie was surely looking down and probably was happier than any-one in town for the way things turned out.

Rebecca was sure different from Josie. She was a small, pretty woman, and her feet were so tiny she could buy up all the sample shoes that were only size five. Uncle Ben thought she was pretty lucky 'cause those sample shoes hardly cost anything. She always wore neat little aprons over her dresses even when she was-n't cooking something. I never saw her in pants or overalls, and I don't think anyone ever saw her without her makeup and earrings. Yep, she sure was different from Josie, but her life wasn't one bit better.

My aunt used to say, "Poor Becky; she gave up so much." But my aunt really wasn't talking about all the money her family had or all the special things like private schools, fancy balls, and trips to Europe that she and her two sisters had enjoyed. When my aunt talked about Becky giving up so much, she was talking about the fact that she had no more family. From the day that Rebecca married Hank, her whole family gave up on her, just pretended she didn't exist. When the grown-ups mentioned it, they called it "dis-owned." I thought that was kind of funny 'cause I didn't know that parents even owned their kids.

Hank was pretty handsome. In fact, people used to say he was the nicest-looking man around, but being in the Navy meant he really wasn't around all that much. I saw Hank only once or twice. He had dark curly hair and bright blue eyes and, like Mrs. Walden, always looked as though he'd been in the sun a lot. The thing I remember the most was how tall he looked. I guess he wasn't much over six feet, but when he stood next to Becky, he sure did look taller than that. Not only was he a sailor; he also was a damned good ballplayer. At least that's what everyone in town said. He didn't play baseball for a big team, just one of the other teams that were one step down. That didn't seem to matter much, 'cause everybody thought he'd be called up soon. They used to talk about how he'd make our little town famous once that happened. I really didn't quite understand it all but sure knew the town was counting on him, probably because there wasn't much else to count on.

I think it was when Becky watched him play ball that she got hooked, but she wasn't the only one. A lot of girls got hooked on Hank, and he sure didn't mind that one bit. In fact, before he and Becky got married, he had a lot of girls, but after that he had only a few extra ones. I used to hear my aunt and Mrs. Walden talking about it. They thought he grabbed on to Becky just to show her parents a thing or two, and both of them wished with their whole heart that he'd grabbed on to one of the others.

Becky lived in a pink house with soft yellow shutters. My aunt said it was a Victorian. All I knew was it sure was different from all the other white houses with black shutters that filled most of the town. I loved to go with my aunt when she went to visit Becky. It seemed like a special place where I could pretend I was rich or something. The kitchen was small, bright, and cheery with colored wallpaper and a table that was always set with a nice cloth, napkins, and two place settings. When she and my aunt would have coffee, she'd carefully take everything off the table and fold up the cloth and napkins, but just as we'd be leaving, she set it up all over again. I guess Becky kept it that way in case Hank should show up any minute. My aunt said that with Hank, you never could tell, but as far as she was concerned, Becky would be better off if he never showed up at all.

The house had a second floor, but on the first floor was a bedroom and bathroom, and that's mostly where Becky lived. There was also the parlor—my favorite of all. It was huge and filled with beautiful things: nice furniture, a lot of knick knacks, and books on shelves that lined each side of a fireplace that really worked. There were other personal treasures, not a single one from the dump.

The window sort of curved around, and underneath those windows was a soft plush window seat where I spent a lot of time, and across from the window on the opposite wall was a piano.

Sometimes Becky would take a break from the kitchen to play a tune. She said that if I wanted to take piano lessons, I could come there every day to practice. I told Becky the only person I knew who could play the piano was Della's ma, and I knew for sure my aunt wouldn't let me go there to learn anything. She told me to never mind; someday when I was a little older, she would try to teach me herself. Of course, that never happened.

Although my aunt wasn't sure I should be alone in the parlor, Becky said I could be there anytime I wanted, so that's just where I went. I was careful not to touch anything, just look. I spent one whole morning just counting books and treasures, but other than that, I just danced around singing to myself and pretending. Boy, could I pretend, but it worked out well; they didn't interrupt my make-believe, and I didn't interrupt their gabbing in the kitchen. Sometimes when I was singing in the parlor, I could hear Becky humming in the kitchen. She sure loved music and always hummed while she fixed the coffee or the plate of goodies she said was necessary so that she could entertain us properly. I was never able to recognize the songs she was humming. I guess they were just tunes she remembered from her different life.

The visits at first were only on Saturdays. I know my aunt planned it that way so that I could go along. Then Becky got sick, and everything changed. At first my aunt went over every other day just to check on Becky and see if there was anything she could do. But when Becky got sicker and sicker, my aunt went every day. She'd go in the mornings and help Becky dress, fix her soup or something like that for lunch, and leave something for her to nibble on at suppertime. It wasn't too long before Becky didn't even get dressed anymore. In fact, there were times when my aunt had to struggle just to get her to change her nightie or get her faced washed. Things just went from bad to worse, and the worst part was Becky just giving up on everything. My aunt just didn't know what to do anymore, but she sure knew that somebody needed to be with Becky all the time. I guess that's why she was so glad when Esther, right out of the blue, offered to help.

My aunt would be there right after I left for school in the morning, fix lunch, and stay with Becky until it was time for me to get back to the boardinghouse. Then it would be Esther's turn.

She'd stay until eight or nine o'clock when Becky was asleep for the night. They also rigged up the phone so that Becky could call for either one of them when they weren't around. It sure sounded like a good plan, but when my aunt explained it to Mrs. Walden, she just shook her head, clucked her tongue, and mumbled, "A mistake, a big mistake." But she wouldn't say anything more. She sure knew Esther better than my aunt did.

After just a couple of weeks, Esther told my aunt that she had a friend Ruth, who was a nurse in a neighboring city. She told her that her friend felt so sorry for the situation that she'd be willing to come and sleep over. That way Becky would have around-the-clock care, and the two of them could rest a little easier. At first it seemed to be okay, but it wasn't too long before my aunt began to question a lot of things. Her wondering began the first time Hank showed up.

He didn't come home very often, but when he did show up, those two women were all over him, telling him how wonderful he was and how they felt bad for all he was suffering through. Of course, that made my aunt angry. It wasn't Hank who was suffering; it was Becky. I heard her telling Uncle Ben she thought that instead of feeling sorry for Hank, they should have kicked his ass out of the house. She said Becky was a lot better off when he didn't come around, 'cause he was just a mean bastard who treated her as if she were a big nothing.

He'd tell her she was just a phony, a little, spoiled rich bitch. He'd yell at her, tell her to get the hell out of that bed, and "get over this shit." I did know cancer was shit, but I sure didn't know how you just got over it.

Then things began to be missing. My aunt noticed it first when she convinced Becky she might feel a little better, a little more like her old self, if she let my aunt put on some makeup for her and perhaps a pair of earrings. Becky agreed, but there were no earrings to be found. My aunt went through all three jewelry boxes, the nightstands, and every other place she could think of and there wasn't a single pair of earrings anywhere. When she questioned Esther and her good friend Ruth, they just looked at her with a blank stare and suggested that Hank probably took them the last time he was home. My aunt thought she knew better but really couldn't be sure.

Aunt Harriet and Me

It was another three weeks before Hank showed up again, and in the meantime, other things went missing. I hadn't been allowed over to Becky's in a long time. My aunt wasn't afraid I'd catch anything or anything like that; she just didn't know how I'd take to seeing Becky so sick. But one day she surprised me when she asked me to go along. Walking over, she explained she had something special for me to do—a big, kind of like secret mission. She wondered if I would go into the parlor and spend the morning counting books and treasures the way I did before. I was some excited, but it sure didn't take me all morning to do the counting this time, 'cause there wasn't much left to count. The figurines, little statutes, the beautiful music box that I'd never dared to play, and even some of the books weren't there anymore. It made me very sad because I knew these were special things that Becky had collected when she traveled all over the place with her blue-blooded family. But it didn't make my aunt sad when I told her on the way home; it just made her rip-roaring mad. She waited for Esther and Ruth to show up the next day and then asked them both to come outside where Becky couldn't hear and blasted the hell out of them. She accused them of stealing everything, even the earrings, but they didn't admit to a thing. They stood there smirking at my aunt and saying that Becky had told them to take whatever they wanted because they were so nice to her. They also suggested that if my aunt didn't believe them, she could just go ask Becky. They knew my aunt wouldn't do that; there was no way she would upset her dying friend, and there was no other way she could prove a thing. My aunt knew they were liars and thieves, which she said usually go together anyway. But I guess just because you know something doesn't mean you can do anything about it, 'cause there didn't seem to be much my aunt could do.

Back at the boardinghouse, she'd rant and rave, but that was about it. My aunt did think about calling in the sheriff, but Charlie told her it wouldn't do a damned bit of good. The sheriff was an asshole buddy of Esther's and probably even had one or two of those treasures himself. All he would do is badger poor Becky. And because she wasn't even from around here, he'd enjoy every minute of it. I think my aunt was kind of sorry she ranted and raved about the whole situation, 'cause for a whole week all Charlie did was go on ranting and raving even worse than she did. Sometimes he'd be talking about poor Becky, and then he'd go on and on about Old Joe's daughter. All Mrs. Walden said was, "I'm not surprised" and "I could have told you so."

It was right after my counting visit to Becky's that I first saw Old Man Walden—saw him as clear as could be standing right at the foot of my bed. I really couldn't describe his face, because it was kind of fuzzy, but I could see he was dressed in an old pair of pants with suspenders and a plaid-looking shirt. That much I could tell my aunt once I stopped screaming.

She came rushing into my room, held me, and told me it was just a bad dream. Of course, she blamed herself for taking me to Becky's, her being so sick and all. I sure knew I wasn't going back to Becky's again, but that didn't matter much; I still had those same bad dreams three nights in a row. Finally Uncle Ben suggested and my aunt agreed to leave the doors open between our rooms. Then she took the big picture of the guardian angel off her wall and hung it in my room. It didn't matter to me that it looked too big for where she'd hung it or that it left a big, dark-rimmed white square above her bed; I was just mighty glad to have it. I don't know if it were the open doors, the big picture, or Uncle Ben's loud snoring and farting that kept the old man away, but I never saw him again, at least not at the foot of my bed.

I heard my aunt tell Mrs. Walden that Hank was back, nastier than ever. She thought the fact that he wasn't going to be a baseball star after all, wasn't going to put the town on the map, might have just added to his meanness. I heard them talking about the time he had kicked Becky when he was wearing those damned baseball shoes—kicked her right in the small of her back and hurt her so badly she had to take to her bed for a couple of days. They thought that perhaps they were the only people in town who didn't give a damn if he were some kind of a sports hero or not. They were just happy he'd have to be giving up those shoes. My aunt said it was kind of like "poetic justice," whatever that meant.

They weren't the only ones who didn't care. Charlie didn't care, either. In fact, he was as happy as a pig in shit when he heard. He always thought Hank was a phony. He talked about him as a big phony with a big ego, a bully with a bullshit attitude, and couldn't for the life of him understand why those idiots in the rest of the town couldn't see it.

Hank said he didn't give a damn, either. He was ready and willing to tell anyone who was ready to listen just how it all happened. By the time Hank stopped spreading his story all around town, Charlie had given him one more name, "crybaby shit." Hank said everyone was out to get him. His teammates didn't like him, because he was the best player on the team, and they all knew he would be the first one called to go play big time. He said that the umpires never gave him any fair calls and that the guy who ran the team didn't like him for marrying Becky. Nobody knew for sure what that had to do with anything, but somehow Hank was convinced that whom he had married was part of the problem. Everyone around him caused him trouble. Some people believed him, but, boy, nobody at the boardinghouse did—not my aunt, not my uncle, not Mrs. Walden, but most of all, not Charlie. It was Charlie who found out what really happened and told us one night at suppertime.

He said Hank was right about one thing: that nobody liked him because he took his mean streak right out onto the ball field. But that's not what did him in. It was his drinking that did it. He had been warned over and over but still showed up at practice half in the bag. Then one day during a real game, he'd had enough to drink and really couldn't tell his ass from a hole in the ground. At bat he took a real hard swing at the ball and missed it by a mile. That didn't seem to matter to Hank; he threw down his bat and tried to race to the bases just as if he'd gotten a home run or something. When they threw him out of the game, he tried to beat up the umpire. That's when they kicked him off the team.

Charlie was sure pleased with himself that he'd gotten the whole story, and it was a story that put Willy and Sam into fits of laughter. For some reason, they kind of liked Hank a little better after they heard it. Uncle Ben thought it was a sorry thing that Hank had given up a chance to make big money just because he couldn't keep himself sober.

The next time Hank left town, nobody saw him again for more than a year and a half. He didn't even come home when Becky died. My aunt thought it was interesting that at the end, Becky never asked for Hank, but she sure was sad when she could hear Becky calling over and over for her mother and her sisters. My aunt telephoned them a couple of times pleading for them to come for Becky's sake. The first time, they claimed they didn't know any Becky. The second time, they admitted that they used to know a Becky but that she had been dead for a long time.

My aunt used to tell me it was always the best to tell the truth, but I guess there are times when it doesn't hurt to lie a little—maybe even lie a lot. This was a time when my aunt lied a lot. Over and over, she'd lie to Becky, telling her that her mother and sisters were coming, that they'd soon be there. She told me that in some cases, lying was all right, especially if it gave someone comfort. Now I guess it would be up to me to figure out when I could lie and when I couldn't. At the end, my Uncle Ben and Mrs. Walden took to watching me because my aunt spent day and night with Becky. She didn't want Esther or Ruth anywhere near the place stealing more stuff and maybe even telling Becky the real truth about her mother and sisters. If it hadn't been for Aunt Harriet, Becky would have died alone.

The guys from the funeral home set up Becky's casket in the parlor, under the windows and right in front of my favorite window seat. She was supposed to stay there for a couple of days so that people, even those who didn't ever bother to come by when she was alive, could come now and see her dead. But a big old blizzard sure did change those plans. It was almost a week before they could get through to take her away. My aunt stayed there day and night—not that Becky needed her anymore; she just didn't think it right to leave her alone. It was school vacation, and with Uncle Ben working and Mrs. Walden really busy, my aunt felt she had no choice but to take me with her during the day. I went only one day and then pleaded with my aunt to leave me back at the boardinghouse. I promised I would not go in the kitchen, visit with ugly old Emma in the parlor and answer her stupid questions about Becky and Hank, or anything. I would stay in my room, even if Old Man Walden was at the foot of my bed, but I sure didn't want to go back to Becky's. My aunt thought she understood, but she really didn't; she had no idea what I had done.

I didn't mean any harm, and I am not even sure why I did it, but while my aunt was cleaning up Becky's room, I crept into the parlor. For the longest while, I just stood there staring at the casket and Becky. Then I got a small stool, stood on it, picked the pennies off her eyes, and tried to open her eyelids. I just wanted to peek inside to see if I could see anything. Maybe I thought I might be able to see some of her blue blood—I didn't know, but I sure knew what I was doing wasn't very nice. I also thought for certain that if I went back there, Becky's ghost would be after me. I didn't go back to that pink Victorian until three years later. I stood there staring at the paint that was peeling and the shutters that had been broken by winter storms.

Good Riddance, Old Man Walden

I didn't have to worry about Becky haunting me, but Old Man Walden was a different story. I began to see him almost every day. He never showed up at the foot of my bed again, probably because of the angel picture, but he sure did wander the halls. The next time I saw him, he was just kind of hanging around down at the end by Emma's room. I sure got out of there in a hurry. My feet were racing almost as much as my gut was. Down the stairs I flew until my aunt grabbed me and told me to stop running or I'd kill myself. I knew that when I told her what I saw, she'd know I wasn't just having a bad dream. It was the middle of the morning, so how could I be dreaming being wide awake and all? Instead, she just told me I was seeing things. It was my imagination. She also told me never— and she meant never—to say anything about this foolishness to Mrs. Walden. I didn't know what I'd do if I ever saw him again. I sure wouldn't tell my aunt, because it made her kind of mad at me. Maybe next time—if there was a next time, and I hoped to God not—I'd tell Charlie. I knew Charlie would listen, and he sure did.

He not only listened; he believed me. He told me that I wasn't just going soft in the head, that the old man was really hanging around. He said things in his room often got moved around, sometimes just a little bit—like a statue or cup and saucer wouldn't be on his bureau as he'd left them. Then other times the old man really made a mess. One time he found his books scattered all over the place instead of in a neat pile in the corner. He wasn't afraid, though; he'd just straighten things out and say out loud, "For Christ sakes, leave my things alone." He'd never really seen the old man, but he sure knew he was there for some reason or another. He told me that the next time I saw him, I should just shout, "Get out! Leave us alone!" and then say a little prayer.

I could sure do the "get out" part but wasn't sure I knew just what do to about a prayer. That's when I decided to tell my friend Little Mary Theresa. She knew about werewolves, ghosts, and stuff because of her brothers, and because of her mother, she sure knew all about prayers. It took us awhile to come up with a good one. It started "Dear God," because Little Mary Theresa said you always start a prayer with that, and then went on:

"Dear God, make the old man go away.

"Don't let him come back another day.

"Tell him to leave us alone

"And get his ass out of my home.

"Amen."

The last line was my idea, and although my friend didn't know if God would like it or not, I said we had to keep it there, and she was so proud of helping me that she stopped complaining.

At recess time we'd go to the corner of the playground and say it together over and over and then cross ourselves. That's another thing that Little Mary Theresa said we had to do. After saying "amen," you always had to cross yourself. The teachers noticed, but I was glad they didn't say anything or ask any questions. They might not have liked the "ass" part, either. I guess they just thought that it was something Little Mary Theresa's mother told her she had to do at recess time and that I was just doing it with her 'cause she was my friend. That sure was okay with me. But even with all the practice, the next time I saw the old man, I forgot most of our prayer. All I could remember was "get your ass out of my home." I even forgot to say "amen" or cross myself. So I guess it was really Aunt Harriet who finally drove him away.

I saw her standing in front of the door that led to the third floor. She kept tugging at it to see if she could open it, but it was locked solid, just like always. At her feet was what I thought was a bunch of different-colored rags, but it wasn't. It was an old Indian blanket. "This has to end!" she said. "Enough is enough! Do you hear me?" she said over and over again. "Enough is enough!" Then she took the blanket, wrapped it in newspaper, and that night gave it to Uncle Ben to take to the mill. She told him not to ask any questions, "just take the damned thing and throw it into one of the furnaces." Then she told me once again not to mention this to any-one—not Charlie, not Emma, and especially not Mrs. Walden. I was really glad she hadn't mentioned Little Mary Theresa, 'cause I sure had to tell her. The next thing my aunt did was to hug me and tell that there are times when young people can see things the older folks can't and that if I ever saw the old man again, I should be sure to tell her. But I never saw him again, not even one more time, even though I tried to.

I guess now that my aunt believed me and was like on my side, I wasn't really scared the way I used to be. I guess I kind of wanted to try the whole prayer just once to see what would happen. I never had that chance. In fact, I couldn't even hear him stomping around the third-floor attic anymore. When I told Little Mary Theresa, she said that what I should do now was just say, "Amen, amen," every time I went to my room or walked past that third-floor door and cross myself. "Don't forget to cross yourself," she warned. I did that for about one whole week and then just got tired of it. So that was that for me, and that was that for the old man.

Della and Her Family Move In

Things were pretty quiet after that until Della and her whole family moved into the boardinghouse barn. They had to live there for a couple of months while Della's pa and some guys from town fixed up their house after the fire.

It was the first time that Della or any of her family, except for her pa, had ever stayed away from home. Her pa had been gone for three months one time. He went to live with a lady named Grace down in the Dirty Dozen. Her husband had been killed in a mill accident, and Della's pa felt so sorry for her he moved in just to give her some comfort. Della didn't talk too much about it, and she said her ma never mentioned it at all. Then one day out of the clear blue sky, her pa just came marching back in. Della said she guessed her ma was kind of glad, because she couldn't handle the boys all by herself. They used to bug her to death. Sometimes they wouldn't get up to go to school, they never helped with the chores, they made the girls miserable, and they used swear words all the time. They couldn't say one full sentence without some swear words. As near as I could tell, it wasn't much different from when their pa was at home. Della also guessed her pa would have stayed with Grace forever if she hadn't found some other guy who could comfort her better.

Her pa made the whole family tell everyone the fire started when the barn got hit by lightning. That sure was hard to believe, because there hadn't been any storms for miles around, but that was their story, and they stuck to it—all except Della, who told me the real story just a couple of weeks after they moved in.

Her brothers had this great big scheme where they thought they could blow up the shit in the outhouse. They made bomb like things out of hay and scraps of paper and other stuff, and then they would set them on fire and throw them down the hole. Except for getting splashed with some smelly stuff nothing much happened, their bombs just sort of fizzled and sunk. I guess they didn't realize that shit doesn't burn too well. But they wouldn't give up; they just kept building bigger bomb things until they built one that was too big to fit down the hole. They didn't even think about that until they had it already burning. The fire caught on to all the stacks of old newspapers and piles of catalogs they used to wipe their behinds and just took off burning the barn, the shed, and a little bit of the house. Nobody was supposed to know the real story, because then Della's pa couldn't collect any money to fix things up.

Della's ma helped Mrs. Walden around the boardinghouse, but that sure didn't make up for the trouble the boys caused, and it sent Kathy right plumb into one of her hissy fits. She threatened to run away to Egypt, but, of course, she never did. She just packed her bag and sat on the porch for the longest time. When Mrs. Walden finally asked her why she was still there, she only shouted, "What's the matter with you, old lady? Can't you take a joke?"

It took Kathy about a week to settle down, but the boys never did. They caused us trouble the whole time they were there. They got into all of Sadie and Shakespeare's stuff, which made Mrs. Walden have a fit almost as bad as one of Kathy's. They sneaked up and down the halls. They got into Charlie's room enough that he put a big padlock on his door. He said it was different when the old man haunted his place. He only moved things around, but these "hoodlums were stealing his shit." They always made fun of Mrs. Walden's cooking. They'd pretend to gag and hold their noses when they came to the table, but that didn't slow down their eating like pigs. No matter what she put on the table, I knew it was better than that old fish hash.

But the worst of all was the way they treated Buster. They'd bump into him on purpose and then laugh and run away. They called him all kinds of names, like "the blind old duffer" and "the mole." They got sticks, and when nobody was watching, they'd just tap, tap, tap in front of Buster's door pretending they couldn't see, either. Buster began to stay in his room a lot, and at supper he'd try to sit between Uncle Ben and Charlie so that maybe they could protect him. When Charlie caught on to what was happening, he took those boys outside and told them if they didn't leave Buster alone, he'd "hang them by their balls right from those G-D barn rafters." After that they eased up a little bit but still called Buster "the mole." I kind of figured the damage had already been done, and because the oldest brother was the worst, I guessed he'd be the one to go blind the day Buster died. I remember Charlie always saying, "What goes around comes around," and he told me many times, especially when he was talking about the Roman Empire thing, that "history repeats itself." I sure didn't want Buster to die right away, but was still kind of anxious to see just what would happen.

There weren't too many guys in town willing to help build back the place. It seemed at first they all had something else to do until Della's pa asked them how they thought their damned kids were going to get to the next out-of-town ball game, and then a whole crowd showed up.

It was kind of fun to have Della at the house. We spent a lot of time together playing jacks and stuff. But at school if she hung around me, Mary Theresa wouldn't. That bothered me some, but what I really worried about was Della telling the kids that a lot of my stories about the boardinghouse was just made-up stuff. She never said a word, and I guess that was because I never told anyone how that lousy fire really got started.

Everyone was pretty happy when they finally moved back home—everyone except Della, who really wanted to stay but couldn't 'cause her ma needed her for chores and things, and Willy and Sam, who said they sure as hell were going to miss those boys. They said the brothers kind of reminded both of them of what they were like when they were younger.

After they left, things went back to the way they used to be. Charlie took the padlock off his door, Buster came out of his room more often, Kathy didn't seem to have much to have hissy fits about, and Emma went right back to talking about all the accidents, murders, and stuff she'd read about. There wasn't much to get excited about until the day Mrs. Walden found Emma dead in bed.

Not Our Emma—Quite the Opposite

Emma never complained about being sick or anything like that, probably because she was too busy complaining about everything else. It was kind of like now you see her, now you don't, so it really was a shocker. Mrs. Walden was running around trying to figure out what to do. It was Aunt Harriet who stepped in and took charge. She knew what had to be done because she'd done all that stuff for Becky. She called for the doctor first because she knew he'd have to come take a look and say, "Yep, she's really dead." Then he'd call for the man at the funeral parlor in the next town over to come and take her away.

Afterward Aunt Harriet went down the street to tell the lady who did Emma's hair that she wouldn't be able to keep her next appointment but wondered if the lady would be kind enough to go to the funeral parlor and do Emma one last time. She told Mrs. Walden to go to Emma's room and find something pretty to bury her in. That was when Mrs. Walden found all those books with the pictures and as many postcards as Kathy had.

The postcards were of places Emma had been in the past, all kinds of places. That surprised everyone but not as much as the pictures did. There were all kinds of pictures, and Emma was smiling in every one of them. In one she was in a long dress, had some flowers on her wrist, and was leaning against a tall man who was handsome in the same way Hank was. There were pictures of her at a beach in a long tank like swimming suit, pictures of her and the man on horseback and on a lawn holding tennis racquets. There was even a picture of her dressed up for a Halloween party. The man was in most of the pictures, but even when he wasn't there, Emma was still smiling. She sure looked happy, and the smiling made her even look pretty. I wished the pictures had been in color instead of just old black and white, and then I could have really seen how pretty that long dress was. Perhaps I could have even seen the red color of Emma's hair when she was much younger.

Mrs. Walden and Aunt Harriet were really quiet as they pored over those pictures. Once in a while one of them would say, "Can you believe this?" or "Oh, my Lord, look here." But mostly they were quiet and looked a little sad. They both wished Emma had shared with them a little bit of what her life had been like. Too late now, but at least they knew what to do for the service.

They took the pictures to the funeral parlor and put them on a table so that everyone could see the "other" Emma. They hoped people would remember her as the smiling one, but I doubted it. If she never smiled at you face to face, then no old picture would do it. It probably didn't matter much, 'cause hardly anybody came, just a handful of people. Everyone from the boardinghouse went, but they were the only ones who sent any flowers. Even Uncle Ben paid for a small bunch.

The lady who did Emma's hair came in with a few other ladies. I think they were just ones who went to the same place to get their hair cut or colored; they weren't really Emma's friends. They didn't spend much time with the pictures. Mostly they just kept looking at her and talking about how good she looked.

My aunt explained exactly what we should do. We were to walk by the casket, look at Emma and say, "Go in peace," and then go sit on one of the folding chairs and say some quiet prayers. Looking at Emma wasn't the hard part. In fact, I didn't feel much of anything. But saying those prayers to myself sure wasn't easy. I tried to say prayers I'd memorized in church, but some of them just didn't fit, like the one "Bless me, Father, for I have sinned."

The chairs were really hard, and the women in front of me kept talking and even laughing. They talked about other dead people they had known. They talked about who in town was sick enough to be the next one to go. They even talked about which husband just up and left. It was like an old-fashioned get-together. Every once in a while they'd stop chatting long enough just to say to one another, "She certainly looks good, doesn't she?" After a while Charlie couldn't stand it another minute. He leaned over and tapped one of them on the shoulder. "Hey, ladies," he said, "this isn't a social event. Save your gossip for the beauty shop or your next little card game. And don't say one more time that she looks good. Jesus, God almighty, there isn't a dead person anywhere that looks good." I guess Charlie and I must think just alike, because I sure don't think dead people look good, either.

I thought my aunt would be as upset as Charlie was, but she wasn't. She wasn't even surprised at all the talking and stuff. She had been to a lot of wakes and said that people often gather in a corner and talk about old times, usually because they hadn't seen one another for quite a while. She wasn't at all surprised about those ladies, but she sure was surprised when Hank walked in, and so was everyone else.

He sure didn't look handsome anymore. He looked really old, kind of scraggly, and dirty, as if he'd been sleeping outdoors. He didn't speak to anyone or even nod. He just slowly went up to the casket, stood there mumbling something over and over, and then walked out. Someone said they thought he might have been in town, because they had seen lights on in the house for the last couple of nights. But no one, including my aunt, who is really smart, could figure out what was going on. He didn't even come to help bury his wife, so what was he doing at Emma's funeral? He hardly even knew her. No one was talking, and I could tell that no one was praying, either. Everybody just seemed confused. It was Charlie who finally said, "We may be a little confused but sure as hell not as confused as Hank is. Poor Hank." It was the only time I ever heard Charlie talk about Hank as if he liked him, even a little bit.

After that day, there were no more lights in the house and no more Hank in town. It was the last anybody ever saw or heard from him. It was a bad thing that was happening with Hank, but because of that, it would eventually be a good thing that would happen to my aunt, my uncle, and me.

There was a brief service, where the skinny old man who owned the funeral house talked about what a kind and wonderful woman Emma was and how she was loved and would be missed. After that we went back to the boardinghouse and had lunch. I wondered if the minister said all those nice things to try to persuade God to let her up instead of making her go down. Who knows? Maybe she was just stuck somewhere in the middle. The one thing he said that was really true was that she would be missed. Believe it or not, everyone in the house missed her in one way or another. She had just always been there, moaning and groaning, whining and complaining, and now she wasn't there anymore. I knew they were thinking about her, because it was a least a couple of weeks before anyone sat in her chair at the head of the table. And whenever they read about some disaster in the paper, someone would say, "Oh, God, would Emma have enjoyed this one."

Mrs. Walden put all the picture books and postcards in the barn along with Sadie and Shakespeare's treasures and some other things that were out there. She thought that someday someone might come around and ask about Emma, and in a couple of months that's just what happened.

He was an old man—at least he looked older than Charlie or Uncle Ben—but he still had a full head of wavy gray hair. He was tall and stood tall wearing a suit and a topcoat, something we didn't see too often around our town. He quietly asked my aunt if she knew where he could find a Mrs. Brady. My aunt just answered that she knew no Mrs. Brady. Then he replied in a quiet tone, "Emma Brady. ... Are you certain you don't know her? I was led to believe she might live here."

"Up until a couple of months ago, we had an Emma Burton here but no Emma Brady."

"What did she look like? Was she warm and friendly, always ready to help others? Did she smile a lot?"

"No, sir, not our Emma. In fact, she was quite the opposite."

"Then I guess that could not have been my Emma," he sighed. "I have been looking so long and so wanted to find her. She was really my only love, and a foolish mistake on my part forced her away. I have only one other question," he said. "What color was her hair?"

But before my aunt even answered, she realized that the old man standing in front of her was the same man she had seen in those pictures. She invited him to have a seat in the parlor and told him she would be back in just a couple of minutes. She told Kathy to bring him a cup of tea, went to the barn to get those picture books, and returned to find him sitting in what we all called "Emma's chair." She spoke to him in a quiet voice. "Before I give you these books, I think I should tell you that our Emma, the one we knew as Emma Burton, was buried two months ago. But I think you had better check these out."

He held those books with shaky hands for a long time before he even turned to the first page. I guess he knew just what he would find inside. Then he began to cry—not crying real loudly or wailing or anything like that, but you sure could tell he was crying. His shoulders were bobbing up and down, and every once in a while he'd clear his throat and wipe his eyes with a really nice handkerchief. The first time he sobbed, "Oh, my God, my Emma," my aunt suggested we just leave him alone in the parlor. Of course, Kathy wanted to stay around, but Aunt Harriet gave her a big shove. In fact, she pushed her all the way into the kitchen, made her sit on a stool, and told her to keep her "snotty, nosey behind right where it was plunked." Kathy sure wasn't happy, but for some reason, she didn't throw one of her hissy fits. Maybe she'd save it for suppertime.

I was very glad to get out of there. That man was making me feel really sad. I never saw a man cry before. In fact, I didn't think they even knew how. Even Willy, when he was pulling out all those teeth, didn't cry. He just swore a lot. My Uncle Ben was just always quiet. Charlie used to rant and rave when he thought something wasn't fair. Willy and Sam used to burp and fart at the table, but that's all I knew about men. I didn't know they cried, and I wondered that if they ever did, would it be quiet crying like the old man in the parlor?

Mrs. Walden finally went into the parlor to ask the man if he'd like something to eat. She also asked if he wanted to stay a night or two, and he just shook his head no to both of her offers. Then she told him there were a couple of boxes with Emma's things in the barn and asked if he'd like them. This time he just mumbled, "No, thank you. The pictures will do." He put on his topcoat, tucked the picture books under his arm, and headed to the depot to wait for the next train out of town. I watched him from the window, and he sure wasn't walking as tall as before. All of a sudden, I wished with my whole heart that Emma hadn't upped and died.

Aunt Harriet and Mrs. Walden talked about him for days. I think they were trying their best to figure out what had happened, but when I asked my aunt what she thought, she just told me to mind my own business. "Whatever happened between the old gentleman and Emma happened years ago and is their own private affair. There is no use dwelling on it."

But that sure didn't keep my aunt and Mrs. Walden from dwelling. It took a couple of weeks before they let it go. That was after they both had decided they liked the old gentleman. If he'd made a mistake, Emma should have been a little more forgiving. That would have been good for him but even better for Emma. They said maybe her last years wouldn't have been filled with so much bitterness and anger. If she had been the Emma that the old gentleman described, then people would have liked her better. I thought, "Maybe if she could have smiled just a little like she had in all those pictures, we'd all have a different Emma to remember."

Boardinghouse or Bug House?

I never missed much school. Aunt Harriet kept telling me over and over how important school was. That meant a cold or a runny nose or any little thing like that wouldn't get me a day off. She used to tell me that my going to school was just like Uncle Ben going to work. It was my job. I guessed that if I got really sick, she'd probably let me out of going, because sometimes when Uncle Ben was really sick and went to work anyway, she'd bitch at him. She'd tell him he should stay home and stay in bed, but, of course, he never listened. I knew I sure would, and I got my chance when I came down with the chicken pox.

I had a very little case, so it wasn't all that bad except for the itching. My aunt made me stay in bed, brought me soup and cookies, and read me books. She sure did fuss over me, and every few minutes she was dabbing those little blisters with a paste made out of baking soda and water. She tried to make sure I didn't do any scratching, but, of course, whenever she left the room, I scratched and scratched, not only because of the itching, but because I really wanted to see if it were true that I could get some scars for life. My aunt was just so kind and caring when I had those chicken pox that I guess I expected she would be the same when I came home from school with bugs. Believe me, she wasn't; instead, she was just mad as hell.

She had told me more than once not to try on other people's hats or coats, especially the hats. But sometimes at recess, we used to dress up in each other's clothes just for the fun of it. Recess was a pretty short time, so I couldn't believe anything could happen, and who knew about bugs anyway?

It was at supper when I was digging my head in between

bites that Mrs. Walden suggested that perhaps she and my aunt should have a look. They sat me on a stool and began looking through my hair, and then both shouted at the same time, "Oh, my God. She is loaded!" I didn't know for sure if that was good or bad.

Mrs. Walden suggested the only thing they could do was put kerosene on my head and wrap it in a big old towel, and that's just what they did. I sure didn't like it but knew I better not say so. Now I was to supposed to sit for a good, long time all wrapped up like that. First my whole head started to tingle, and then it started to burn. That's when I started to cry, soft like at first and then into a big old yowl. Man, did I ever make a racket. I yelled loudly enough that they finally decided to unwrap me. That was a pretty good thing; my scalp was all red, and I was about to get me some big old blisters.

Next came the combing, which didn't work well at all. They had this little, tiny tool that was supposed to be a comb but sure didn't look like anything I'd ever used before. I guess it didn't help that my hair was pretty long, but my aunt sure took care of that in record time. The bugs were gone, and so was most of my hair.

My aunt kept telling me that the new haircut looked really nice. She said it was awfully cute, but I sure didn't think so. It was short all right, but it had a couple of pieces on each side that made me look as though I had wings or something. Then she suggested that if anyone asked me who cut my hair, I should say the lady down the street did it. If it looked all that nice and all that cute, I couldn't figure out why she didn't want anyone to know that she was the one with the scissors.

I was a little afraid to go back to school, but I shouldn't have been. There were a whole lot of kids with new haircuts, and some were even worse than mine. Even some of the kids who didn't swap hats at recess had haircuts. That made me think that those bugs could probably just jump from desk to desk or head to head.

For a while some of the kids thought I had brought the bugs. A couple of them even began calling the boardinghouse the Bug House. They thought I had probably gotten them from dirty old Willy or Sam. That wasn't the truth, but it sure made me sad. Little Mary Theresa took my side because she didn't like kids picking on other kids, especially if the other kid was her best friend. She was like that. Della took my side, too. She told the smart alecks that I never got close to Willy or Sam, that I even sat on the opposite side of the table at suppertime. She said she knew because she had lived there. She really let them have it, and after a while they shut up.

I wasn't so sure why she fought so hard unless she knew who had the bugs first. I wasn't sure, but all I knew was the next time I saw Della's ma, she even had a haircut just like the rest of us. I asked my aunt if she thought bugs could come from chickens. She just told me no, but she never told me where they did come from. That made me be extra careful. I vowed I would never borrow anyone's hat or coat again. In fact, I wouldn't even borrow a pencil.

A Bad, Dark Secret

I learned a little later that it wasn't just the bugs that made my aunt angry and act a little mean. She knew something bad—really bad—about Willy and Sam but didn't tell anyone. She was just keeping it to herself, worrying about it, at the same time those damned bugs came along.

As the story went, it was late one very cold night when my aunt was alone in the kitchen. She had just come down from her room to fix a cup of warm milk to help her sleep when Willy and Sam came slamming in, drunk as skunks. Sam went straight up to his room—well, maybe not straight up, 'cause he did a lot of swaying side to side. It was up two steps then down two steps until he got to where he could do two steps up and only one step down. But Willy wasn't going anywhere until he told his story to Aunt Harriet.

He said that after the bar closed, they decided to go pay a visit to an old man named Tom Howard, who lived in a little old shack not too far out of town. One of the shack's two windows was covered with tar paper, the door didn't quite close tightly, and there were plenty of cracks in his walls. Tom had a table, a couple of chairs, a cot, and a big old wood stove, and that was it. But everyone in town knew that Tom had something else: a lot of home brew that he had hidden all over the place. And that's just what Willy and Sam were after.

Willy said they were prowling around outside just as quiet as they could be. But as drunk as they were, they probably weren't being as quiet as they thought. Anyway, old Tom woke up, came outside, and tried to chase them off his property. He had been drinking some of his own stuff, so he probably wasn't in much better shape than the two of them were. But that sure didn't excuse what happened next. Willy said they had gotten into a rip-roaring argument over where the brew was hidden, and he finally decked Tom a good one—knocked him out cold. That probably hadn't been too hard to do, because Willy was much bigger and much younger than little old Tom. Then, he told my aunt, came the funny part.

They decided as a joke to strip Tom naked and throw him inside on the cot. They figured when he woke up, he'd wonder what the hell happened. For some stupid reason, Willy thought that was pretty damned funny. They looked around some more but didn't find a single jug of home brew, so they just left and made their way back to the boardinghouse. "End of story," Willy told Aunt Harriet. "End of story," he said, still laughing. But it sure wasn't.

Two days later the sheriff was going around asking questions of almost everyone in town. Just before he got to Mrs. W's place, Willy grabbed my aunt in the upstairs hall and kept telling her over and over that his story about them being up at Tom's was a big lie—that nothing like what he told her really happened and that they hadn't been anywhere near Tom's place. My Aunt Harriet had no idea what was going on, but she found out soon enough.

Someone had found poor old Tom dead on his cot. He was naked and frozen to death. "Frozen stiff," the sheriff said. The sheriff asked questions of everyone there except Buster and my aunt. For some reason, he never asked Aunt Harriet a single question, so she didn't volunteer any answers. She said she had no idea why she didn't speak up. She said over and over again that if the sheriff had asked her, she would have told him the story Willy had told her. But he didn't ask, so she didn't tell.

Keeping a secret like that really troubled her, but when she confided in Uncle Ben a few days later, he just told her to let it be, so she did. But that sure didn't mean that she wasn't still troubled. She told me this story a time later when she said she had another secret she said troubled her even more, a secret she really needed to share with me. She said someday she'd tell me—someday when the time was right.

Julia's Story

Julia moved into Emma's old room, and what a delight she was. She was a small, bubbly, cute little lady who kept us all laughing. She was kind to Buster, helpful to Mrs. W, and a good friend to my aunt. In fact, they acted as if they had been friends forever. She really adored Charlie, and she was the only one I ever knew who could bring Kathy out of one of her hissy fits real quick like. As for Willy and Sam, she was always polite and pleasant but managed to keep her distance.

She never had a bad word to say about or to anyone, and I don't think she even knew how to whine. If she did, I never heard her. For her, everything was always wonderful. Each day she found something new to appreciate. And each day she greeted me when I came home from school with a big "Well, hello, sweetie." Then we would talk about everything that happened. She'd ask me about my teachers, my friends, what we had for lunch, what we did at recess, and she'd always ask if I needed any help with my homework. Every once in a while she'd tell me a funny story. One time she said she knew a lady who used to send her laundry down the street to the Chinese laundry. One day when her bloomers came back a little dirty, she wrote a note to the laundryman. She wanted to make sure he understood, so she wrote, "Pleasee use more soapee on the panties." But he wrote back, "You pleasee use more paper on the poopee."

My friends at school really loved that one, and sometimes at recess we'd grab hands, form a circle, and run around singing, "Soapee on the panties," until someone yelled, "Switch!" and then we'd go in the other direction singing, "Paper on the poopee." It was a great new game and lasted quite awhile. I was real glad she told me stories, because not much was happening at Mrs. W's, and I was kind of running out of things to make up to tell at school.

One time she even told me a little dirty joke. She asked, "Do you know what the little girl mouse said to the little boy mouse?" Of course, I didn't, so she told me. "The little girl mouse told the little boy mouse, 'If you come over here, I'll show you my hole.' "

I thought that was pretty funny, but my Aunt Harriet sure didn't. She didn't get mad at Julia the way she would have at Emma. She just told her, with a smile on her face, "No more jokes." I was kind of disappointed, especially when my aunt told me I shouldn't repeat that one. She said it really wasn't the kind of thing that kids should be listening to on school grounds. I wanted to tell her about Della's brothers and their friends and some of the things they said and did—like sometimes when we were playing our ring-around-the-soapee-poopee game, they would get in a circle and shout, "Ham and eggs between your legs, pork chops and gravy. Old Ma works, old Pa jerks, and out pops a baby." I just figured that if they could say that, then I sure could tell my mouse joke. And besides, I had to have at least one good one I could tell. We tried to think up a "show me your hole" game, but nothing seemed to work, and when Little Mary Theresa got so upset she started to cry, we just dropped the whole idea.

Suppertimes were not at all what they used to be—just eat and go. Now we sat around the table for a long while listening to Julia. She not only told us funny little stories; she also talked about her life and how good it had been, but some of it sure didn't sound all that good to me.

She told us she was the youngest of five children. There were two older brothers and two older sisters. She thought one of her brothers was a real genius; he never studied but was always tops in his class. He could read a book in no time at all and remember exactly what was on page after page. During his senior year in high school, he got offers from colleges all over the place, but two months before graduation, he just dropped out of school—just dropped out for no reason. All he said was that he dropped out because he wanted to and that nobody could change his mind. She said he was real stubborn, just like most of her family, especially her grandfather. He spent the rest of his life doing odd jobs but mostly working as a woodchopper. Every spare minute he had, he spent inventing things. She said he had some really good ideas but was never able to get them off the ground. It was as though nobody wanted to listen. People always thought his life was such a waste, but not Julia. She thought that if what he was doing made him happy, if he was where he wanted to be, doing what he wanted to do, then it wasn't a waste at all.

Julia's mother had given birth to her brothers and sisters right there in the bedroom at the back side of their little one-story house. I guess they did that a lot if you lived in the country, especially in those days. Everyone said her mother had a pretty easy time of it with the other four, but with Julia it wasn't one of those automatic easy things. With Julia it hadn't worked that way at all. Her mother was older, and five years had passed since her last child. It seems that everything that could go wrong went wrong. By the time her father decided to give in and go for the doctor, it was just a little too late. Julia came into the world at the same time her mother left it.

Her father couldn't take care of all those kids, especially with a new baby, so he had to find someplace to go where there would be help. His own people refused. They didn't have room is what they said. Besides, they kind of blamed him for not going for the doctor sooner. They really thought he'd gotten just what he deserved. The only other choice was to go to Julia's mother's folks. They weren't too happy about it, kind of also blamed her father, but at least they didn't say no. So he took his whole brood off to the big old farmhouse.

When she described the farm as a big old rambling place with a wraparound porch, I said it must have looked a lot like the boardinghouse, but Julia said it was quite different. It was far out of town, sat up on a hill, and always looked as if it needed a good coat of paint. There was no dining room, just a big old kitchen where they all ate their meals. There were only two floors but enough bedrooms so that her brothers had one of their own with real beds, and so did the girls. There was a bedroom for her grandparents, a spare one, and one for her father that she said he hardly ever used. There was a parlor that nobody ever used unless company came. As far as I could tell from Julia's story, the preacher who showed up every once in a while was the only real company they ever had.

There were a lot of aunts and uncles and cousins, but they didn't come by very often because they weren't made to feel as though they were welcome. They always sat in the kitchen and stayed only long enough to say a quick hello and drop off bags of stuff they thought the kids could use. That was fine with her granny because she didn't like company anyway, and her grampa said he was too damned busy to waste time with visitors.

The only relatives who didn't drop by were those who had turned Catholic. Not only weren't they allowed in the house, but her grampa said he'd "shoot the ass off any one of them that even dared set foot on my property." Julia said that when she was really young, she wasn't sure what being a Catholic really meant. For the longest while, she just thought it must be something really bad and even wondered if people who turned into one would look different on the outside. She only knew for certain that her grampa meant just what he said. If any of those Catholics dared to stop by, there would be pieces of Catholic asses all over the yard.

The barn was even bigger than the house and wasn't painted white but a dark red. It always looked in better shape than the house because it got painted whenever her grampa thought it needed it. That's where they kept a whole bunch of cows and a couple of work horses, and in the back was a coop for lots of chickens. I asked if the chicken ever came into the house like at Della's. Julia just laughed and said her chickens were strictly outdoor chickens. There were two outhouses in the barn, and I couldn't help but ask if one was for the boys and the other for the girls. Again Julia laughed and said it didn't make a difference one way or the other.

They also had a hog pen right out in back of the barn. She said that when the hogs got big and fat, they sold some and kept some to slaughter and save for themselves. I didn't think there was any difference between a hog and a pig, so I kept thinking about Josie's pig money. I couldn't help but ask Julia how much they got when they sold a batch of them. She said she had no idea but guessed it must have been enough to keep them going.

She said they were always a little poor, but they never went without the necessary things. There was always plenty of good food to eat, and they almost always had decent clothes to wear. The boys could count on hand-me-downs from the cousins who weren't really wanted as visitors. And her granny made skirts, blouses, and dresses for the girls out of the colorful sacks the chicken feed came in. She did say, though, that shoes were sometimes a problem. I really wanted to ask about the shoes part, but my aunt was giving me one of those "You be quiet" looks. I guess she was sick and tired of me interrupting Julia when she was telling a story. But I only asked about the things a kid really needed to know.

Day by day, week by week, we learned more about Julia and what her life had been like. And all through her telling, she did it with a smile on her face. Never once did she act as if she were whining or complaining. I sure hoped that Emma was listening from somewhere.

Julia remembered the fun times she had with her brothers and sisters. They waded in the creek, went fishing, played dodgeball in the field behind the house, and sometimes after supper if it wasn't too late, they'd play kick the can out in front of the barn. In the winter they'd slide using almost anything they could find as sleds. Often the sleds were just old pieces of cardboard. She said those times were really extra special because it wasn't very often that they had time for playing games and such. Mostly they had chores to do.

There were chores before school, after school and on weekends. There were cows to milk, eggs to gather, stalls to clean, and in the summer big gardens to weed and berries to pick. Even the chores didn't seem to be a burden; it was what they were used to, and it was a time when they could talk real loud if they wanted to, a time when they could laugh together or chase each other or the brothers could raise a little hell. It was an outside time when they could act like kids. The time inside the farmhouse was very, very different.

They were expected to be quiet, keep out of the way, and speak only when spoken to. Suppers were probably the hardest for Julia because she always had something she wanted to share, but no one was allowed to speak at the table. I guess that was why Julia most always told her stories at suppertime. If she couldn't talk at the table when she was a kid, she sure as hell could do it now that she was all grown up.

She said that after grace, everybody had to be real quiet. Grampa said it was a time for eating and not gabbing, and speaking out meant you got sent from the table even if you still had a full plate. So they all stayed quiet. She said they also had to wait until everyone had finished eating before a single one of them could move. That wouldn't have worked for Mrs. Walden, because she always started clearing things up before Willy and Sam had stopped stuffing their faces. And it sure wouldn't have worked for me, because it seemed as though I always had to pee right in the middle of supper. Boy, I would have been in deep doo-doo if I had lived there.

Sometimes they sat there for an awfully long time. Her grampa had a big appetite, and many times after he'd cleaned his first plateful, he'd get up walk around a bit, even take a walk outside, to make room for more. Then he'd come back to the table and start all over again. Everybody waited, even her granny. One time she did ask if the kids could get up before he started his second round, and the answer came back loud and clear. "No damned way!"

She said her grandfather was like that. He had ideas all his own about what should be and what shouldn't be, and you just better forget trying to tell him anything different. There was only one right way to gather the eggs, pick the berries, milk the cows, pitch the hay, or shovel the shit. There was only one right way to do just about everything, and that was his way. If he saw Granny sweeping the floor, he'd be apt to grab the broom to show her how she should be doing it. He'd tell her the right way to can the vegetables and fruit and the right way to bake the beans and to sew the dresses. He sure wasn't an easy man to live with, but most of the time when he was out of sight, her granny would go about doing whatever she had to do, however she wanted to do it. And Julia said that's exactly what all the kids did. The only time they followed the rules and did things the so-called right way was when he was standing over them or close by. The rest of the time, they followed their grandmother's example and did whatever they had to do or wanted to do, however they wanted to do it. They were just awfully careful not to get caught.

If that had been me, I would not have liked that stubborn old man, not even a little bit, even if he was feeding me. Julia never said she didn't like him, but then, she never said she liked him, either. She only said he had taught her a lot. At first I thought she meant he'd taught her the right way to do a whole lot of things, like gather the eggs or sweep the floor or stuff like that, but that wasn't it at all. She said that he had taught her tolerance, whatever that meant, and that she learned never to assume that her way of doing things was the right way or the only way. She told me that it was a good lesson for her and that if I thought about it for a little while, I'd surely understand what she meant.

Maybe I would, and maybe I wouldn't. But I knew one thing for sure: I wasn't going to lie awake trying to figure out that tolerance thing. I just lay awake thinking about one stubborn, ugly bastard and how his ghost would be stomping around that old farmhouse trying to get the people who lived there to do things his way.

Julia didn't have too many stories about her father. She told us only that shortly after they all moved into the old farm, he went to a neighboring city to find some kind of job. He went to work in a paper mill, got a room in a boardinghouse, and used the fact that he had no transportation as an excuse for not coming home very often. At first he sent some of his paycheck to help pay for clothes and stuff like that for all his kids, but once he learned that her grandfather used it on other things like paint for the barn, he didn't send it anymore.

Sometimes he'd hitch a ride to visit on a weekend, but as time went by, those visits became shorter and fewer. When he did show up, he'd quietly give some money to her granny, and those were the only times that all the kids would get shoes that really fit or a new coat instead of an old hand-me-down. Of course, Julia couldn't remember his visits when she was real little, but she did remember when he came for her fifth birthday.

It was supposed to be a little party, nothing big, no other kids invited, just her brothers and sisters eating the cake her grandfather told Granny how to make and some homemade ice cream. But, when her grandfather came in from the barn and saw her father at the table, all hell broke loose. At first he just stomped around the table—stomp, stomp, stomp—while the kids just sat quietly. They knew better than to make even a little peep, but not her father. He might have known better, but he spoke anyway.

He tried to explain that he simply wanted to come for Julia's birthday, but that really set the old man off. He began shouting and swearing. "Come home for her goddamned birthday? That's supposed to make you some kind of father? Come here to eat some friggin' cake and ice cream! If you had been a real father, a real man, five years ago instead of some asshole who didn't have any more brains than God gave a biscuit, things would have been a helluva lot different. We would still have our daughter, and you'd be around for all the goddamned birthdays."

"Sorry, Pa. I am really sorry."

"Sorry, my ass. Now get the hell out of here, and don't come back, and don't ever, friggin' ever, call me Pa again!"

Julia said it took her a long time to stop thinking that her father had just dumped them. It took her a long time to understand that her father was a very sad and lonely man who couldn't visit because he wasn't allowed on the property any more than the Catholics were. She knew he cared, because for a while he showed up at her school just to say hello or to give them a little money for something they might need. That lasted only until the grandfather found out. He gave the school people some cock-and-bull story about what was right, what wasn't right, and how things were supposed to be. Either they believed him or, because they knew what he was like, they were afraid not to follow his instructions. That was the end of the school visits. Being the youngest and living at the farm longer than the others, Julia didn't see her father again for years to come.

Her two older sisters married as soon as they graduated from high school. Her brother, the one who wasn't chopping wood or inventing things, went to live in the same boardinghouse as her pa and got a job at the very same mill. He was pretty good with numbers, she said, so he didn't work in the mill part. They gave him a job in the office instead.

People often said they would see her brother and father walking to work together. They would not only be walking, but talking and even laughing. That so upset her grandfather that his favorite name for her brother became "traitor." He swore that if he ever came back, he'd treat him just as he would her father or a

Catholic: He'd shoot his ass off.

The five years she spent after her brother and sisters left were the only lonely times she could really remember. There was really no one to talk to or laugh with. In fact, there was no laughter at all. Her grampa spoke to her only when he felt the need to boss her about something, and her granny—well, her granny was something altogether different.

She remembered how Granny was when they all lived there. She remembered Granny showing them some kindness, sometimes trying to shield them from the ugly old man. She remembered her granny answering questions in a quiet and gentle tone. Even as busy as she was, even with all the struggles, there had been a slight undercurrent of warmth and caring. That's when they had all lived there, but now alone, she found it to be quite different indeed.

Now the questions she asked were either answered in a short, curt way or not answered at all. When she tried to help her grandmother, she was simply pushed aside, told to go do the chores she was expected to do for her grandfather. And so she did, all of them according to his "right way." Even though there had been some little warmth in the past, it had been there for all of them but not especially for her. Thinking back, she could remember now how hard she had worked to please her grandmother. She remembered trying to bring in more eggs or berries than her brothers and sisters did or how carefully she'd tried not spill a drop of milk in the bucket she carried into the kitchen. She didn't cry when she got hurt, didn't grumble about the chores, didn't complain if she was tired, and always sat quiet at the dinner table. She could see now that even as little as she was, she had done, if by some instinct, all of those things to make her grandmother love her. She could also see now that none of those efforts mattered. Nothing she did in the past or could do in the future would make a difference. She was truly alone and unloved and felt it. That didn't mean she would stop trying; in fact, she decided to try all the harder. That didn't work, but Julia said it usually never does.

She kept plugging away, doing very well in school. She wasn't considered a genius like her wood-chopping brother, although she was often compared to him. She was also often encouraged not to turn out the way he did. She had friends at school, but not one ever visited the farm, probably because she never invited them. Growing up, she had clearly gotten the message that visitors weren't really welcome and were no more than a waste of time. So at home, after chores, she read, and read a lot—something she said she never regretted. In fact, she was sure that all that reading was what helped her stay at the top of her class. She had hopes that somehow her grandparents would be proud of her. At night she even prayed that they would notice and say something about how well she was doing, but it never happened. After a while she decided it was probably enough for her simply to be proud of herself.

It was the beginning of her senior year before she got up the courage to ask her grandfather if there was anything she could do to please her granny. "Yep," he said, "stay the hell out of her way. You ain't ever going to please her, and she ain't ever going to love you. She can't; she just can't."

"But why, Grampa, why?"

"Because every time she looks at you, she sees your mother. You look more like her every day that passes, and your granny can't stand the sight of that, and that's why she can't stand the sight of you."

Julia said that at least now she knew. She knew but couldn't for the longest while figure out why that wouldn't have made her granny embrace her rather than reject her. But once she knew, she began to understand the real hurt, the real pain, the real sense of loss her granny was still living with. In years past when there were all those kids to keep in line and mouths to feed, there hadn't been time to hurt. When there was extra work to keep the farm clean and time taken for the figuring of what hand-me-downs would fit who, there wasn't the time to hurt. Worrying about where one of the grandkids would get a pair of shoes that fit or how many skirts or dresses she could get out of the old grain bags she had on hand, there wasn't time to hurt. Julia understood, so her prayers at night were no longer asking that her grandparents notice her and be proud. Now her prayers were for her granny.

It was also at the beginning of her senior year that things began to change for Julia. Her teachers began to "plant seeds," as Julia called it. At first I was trying to picture a garden of some kind right there in the schoolyard, but it wasn't those kinds of seeds. Julia laughed and my aunt frowned when I butted in to ask what they planned on growing. Julia explained the kind of seeds they were planting and that what they wanted to see grow was really just her. That sure mixed me up for a little bit, but after a while I got the hang of what she was telling us.

Two of her teachers, a Miss Goodwin and a Mrs. Leathers, took a special interest in her. They talked to her day after day, telling her she was really too smart to spend the rest of her life on the farm or to just up and get married after graduation. They said there was a whole wide world out there for her to explore and so many experiences she could learn from. After a while Julia really began to listen. She said she realized she had learned a lot of how to be, or how not to be, from living with her grandparents and had already decided marriage sure wasn't something she wanted to jump into without a lot more thought.

There had been a couple of guys in her class who made her heart flutter. She remembered some kissing and hugging behind the school building—enough so that not only did her heart flutter, but her knees got kind of weak and her tummy went to tingling. I really wanted her to tell me more about that kissing and hugging stuff, but she didn't. She simply said that somehow she knew that even though they sure were good at kissing, they probably wouldn't be too good as husbands.

The teachers talked, and Julia listened. They were more than just her teachers; they were her mentors, her friends, and treated her as her mother would have treated her if she'd had a mother. They told her about scholarships that would pay for more schooling and promised her they would see that some came her way. They also asked her to promise she wouldn't say a word about any of these ideas, these seeds they were planting, back at the farm.

Julia thought, Julia dreamed, and Julia prayed. After all, there was more to think about than just scholarships. Where would she live, how would she eat, where would the money come from for books and all kinds of other stuff she'd need? She knew there would be no help from her grampa. In fact, she got a little frightened even thinking that he might learn what she was thinking. She had heard him often enough rant and rave about "jackasses that thought more schooling was called for"—said it was a damned waste of time and money. His view was you did your twelve years, and that was that. In most cases eight years would have been enough; after all, he went to school for only six years, and there wasn't a damned thing he didn't know. Men were supposed to go to work, and women folks were supposed to get married, stay at home, and do what their husbands needed done. And by God, he'd say, those women had better learn to do things the way they should be done, and those weren't things they'd learn in any damned school. Now she wondered if some of that yelling might not have pushed her genius brother to drop out of school and take to the woods.

She knew she wasn't going to drop out of school, get married, or, Lord forbid, take to the woods. So every night she asked for direction, the wisdom to recognize it, and the strength to follow. It was about a month after Julia began thinking, dreaming, and really praying that Miss Goodwin introduced her to her married sister, Lucille Henderson. Julia said that Lucille was the only one of the four Goodwin girls who had managed to snag a husband and that she had caught a damned good one at that. She was also the only one who was as round as she was tall. I couldn't help but ask if she looked a little like Humpty Dumpty, 'cause that's what I was picturing. But Julia said no. In fact, she said she was as pretty as could be. She had blonde, curly hair, a smooth pink-and-white complexion, and a very pretty face. Julia said she was the happiest person she had ever known. I asked if that was because she'd caught a husband and her sisters hadn't. That's when my aunt told me to stop with the questions, but Julia just laughed and answered no. Lucille was just one of those few people who could find something funny in everything. She'd laugh at the drop of a hat, and so would the people around her. She was so pleasant, so delightful, that you soon forgot to notice that she was roly-poly.

Miss Goodwin had gotten Julia excused from a couple of her classes so that she could meet with her and Lucille. Julia had no idea what was up, but she sure could tell that the sisters were excited about something. They marched into the teachers room, and Miss Goodwin just plunked herself in the big old chair that kids sat in when the traveling dentist came to do some teeth checking. She just sat there, arms crossed as if she was hugging herself, and grinning away while Lucille paced back and forth talking ninety miles an hour, explaining who she was and why she had come.

Lucille said she lived in a rather large town about forty-five miles away with her husband, who was a preacher, and four little Hendersons, who were all boys. Julia said she prattled on for more than an hour describing her house, her husband, and her daily routine, and, last but not least, describing her boys. She finally got around to explaining to Julia what in the world this visit was all about. She had an offer for Julia, one she said would be a "cocking good deal for both of them."

Sometimes when Julia was telling a story, she'd stop right at a real interesting part and say she wanted to give someone else a chance to gab a little. That's what she did that night, and when she did, it was almost like waiting for the next chapter of *The Perils of Pauline* to be shown at the grange hall. Pauline was always left tied to the railroad tracks with a train coming, or hanging from a big cliff screaming her head off, or something like that. All of us kids would have to wait a week or two or even sometimes three before we found out if she'd gotten rescued. Of course, she always did, but none of us liked to be left hanging until we found out for sure. That time I was left hanging through two more suppertimes before I got to find out about that "cocking good deal." I thought it was probably more "cocking" for Lucille than it was for Julia, but Julia thought it an answer to all her prayers, so I guess it really was.

There was a normal school within walking distance from the Henderson house. I wondered what a school would be like if it wasn't "normal" but didn't dare ask. I came to find out it was just a school that taught girls how to become teachers. It seemed to me it would have made more sense to call it a teachers school so that folks like me wouldn't get so darned confused. Miss Goodwin had arranged for Julia to get scholarship money for her tuition. And if she were willing to live with the Hendersons and help Lucille just a little around the house, she would get free room and board and a small allowance for books and other stuff she might need.

After Julia told us what it involved, "helping Lucille just a little" sure meant something different from what I thought it would. In the mornings she would fix breakfast and make sure the older boys got ready for school and the little guy was all cleaned up and dressed for the day. Next she packed lunches, did the dishes, and made all the beds. Then she was off to school. If she hurried, she wouldn't be late for her first class, so most mornings she ran all the way. In the afternoon she made sure the boys changed from their school clothes to their play clothes and tried to keep them out of trouble while she fixed the supper. I guess that keeping them out of trouble was the hardest part of all. They threw things down the well, teased the neighbors' girls until they got them crying, threw mud balls at each other, and were always peeing outside. There was no end to what they could think up to do. Lucille always thought that what her boys did was funny, except for the time they set the field on fire.

After supper Julia did the dishes, cleaned up the kitchen, and tried to get the boys settled for bed. Needless to say, they weren't the easiest ones for settling. The only thing she didn't have to do was help them with their prayers. The preacher pa took care of that, but from what I was hearing, it didn't seem to matter who did the prayers; they weren't doing much good anyway. On Saturdays she changed all the beds, did the washing and ironing, and gave the whole house a good cleaning. She said that was the easiest day of all because the Hendersons went visiting just about everyone they knew and took the boys with them. Sundays were not bad days, either. All she had to do was make a big Sunday dinner while everyone was at church and then do the cleaning up. After all of her chores were finished, she was free to go up to her room and do the studying she needed to do.

The house sounded a lot like Becky's, a big old Victorian, except it wasn't painted pink with yellow trim. There was an empty room on the second floor that Lucille said was saved for company, even though they never had any, so Julia's room was way up on the top floor. From the way Julia described it, it didn't sound to me like a room kind of room but just an old attic. She said that after climbing up some steep stairs, you got into her room by pushing up the large board that covered the open space, something like a hatch I guessed. She said the inside was real big and seemed to go on and on, but only one small part was fixed up for her. The other end had all kinds of things stored: old boxes, old pictures, a couple of old mattresses, a rack where Lucille had all her old, ugly maternity clothes hanging, and lots of other stuff. I pictured it as just the kind of place Charlie would love to have gone picking in.

On Julia's side, she said, she had a small bed, a table that she used as a desk, two chairs, and a big old cardboard wardrobe where she could hang her clothes. There was a lightbulb that hung down from the rafters that you turned on by pulling the chain real hard. Julia said she loved her room, and even though it was rather wide open, the way the eaves slanted down made it feel cozy. Of course, you couldn't stand up straight expect in the middle, but none of that seemed to bother Julia. She said that doing the chores didn't bother her, either. She had learned about hard work from living on the farm. And at night when she was lying in bed and heard all the scurrying around at the other end, she knew it was just the mice, and the barn at the farm had gotten her used to them, so that didn't bother her, either. I guess nothing much bothered Julia. The fact that it was real hot up there in the summer and real cold in the winter, and that she had to study with just that small, poor light, weren't things she whined about. She never even complained about her allowance. It was enough to buy the books she needed once she found some secondhand ones. And in the four years she lived there, she even had enough to buy two pairs of shoes that really fit.

She went back to the farm only once in those four years. It was when she got word that her grampa had died. She said it was real odd because she didn't feel much of anything—no grief, no guilt, no sorrow. She felt nothing. It was the preacher and Lucille who insisted she go and pay her last respects, so she went. As she walked up the hill to the farmhouse, she thought back to the day she left. She had really been worried, a little frightened, and had braced herself for the yelling, screaming, and name calling she was sure she was going to get from her grampa, but there had been nothing, not a single word from him or her granny. They had just turned their backs and went on with what they were doing. Somehow she remembered thinking that the silence had been even harder to take. Now she was back.

Visitors who had come to pay their last respects were all gathered around in the parlor, even the ones who were Catholics. I thought maybe the ones who weren't there to gossip or chat or talk about how good the old man looked were probably there so that they'd have a chance to be in that parlor without getting their asses shot off. Julia said she stayed most of the day, got to hug her sisters and their children, and talked to the one brother who worked in the mill office. She was disappointed that her father and her genius wood-chopping brother didn't show up but said she clearly understood. Just as she was ready to leave, her granny called her aside.

"Julia," she said, "I have only one thing to say. You are a very good girl." She said it with tears in her eyes and slowly walked away.

It was the only time in her entire life that her grandmother ever said a kind word to her or about her. I wondered why Julia hadn't answered with something like "Well, it sure in hell is about time," but then I guess that's where that tolerance thing came in.

Night after night Julia had some part of her story to tell. Nobody ever thought her stories were sad ones, because she never told them sad. Whenever my aunt had her ears on Julia instead of her eyes on me, I would eat as fast as a pig in a pen. I didn't want to have a mouthful in case there was a question I needed to ask, and besides, I could hear better if I wasn't chewing.

The Asshole Buddies Share Their Stories, and Kathy Goes on the Wild Side

It wasn't too long before other people started telling some of their stories. Everyone had something to share except for Buster and my aunt and uncle. They just sat quiet most of the time and listened, except when either Willy or Sam tried to put in his two cents' worth. When those two got started, my aunt would soon get up and start to clear the table and my uncle would just go upstairs to his friends Amos and Andy, who he said were a hell of a lot more entertaining.

Willy and Sam had been, as Charlie would say, "asshole buddies" for most of their lives. They seemed to think that their families had been big jokes and that everything they had done was funny as hell. Sam told us that they had grown up in a town that was too small to have a town drunk, so their pas had to take turns. He said that once in a while, one of the old "bastards" would stay sober for three or four days, and that's when the other one could be seen staggering down the street with piss in his pants. The next week it would be the other way around. I guess the word *piss* made Willy remember the time he knocked his old man on his ass. He couldn't remember why he did that but only that he got locked in a closet for a day and a half and found a great way to get even. He said he pissed in all the coat pockets and then shit on the floor and rubbed it all over the walls. He figured that would teach his pa a lesson, but, of course, it didn't. It was his ma who had to clean it all up, and she did it without saying a single word, but, boy, did Sam and Willy laugh. They thought it was real funny, but not as funny as when Sam's pa got mad at the priest and shit on the church steps. "Remember that?" they would ask each other. Always laughing, they remembered a lot of things.

They remembered when they were in school getting swatted

with a rubber hose and also getting their heads banged against the blackboard. They got sent home time and time again and just loved it, especially when the drunks they had as fathers always thought it was the teacher's fault. Sam said he had hoped in the worst way that his pa would find a reason to go shit on the school steps, just as he had done on the church steps when he was pissed at the priest, but it never happened. They might have been sent home, but, of course, they never went there. A day off just gave them a chance to hang out and raise a little hell.

Sometimes they would hike to the neighboring town and shoplift a little—never took very much, just a couple of doughnuts or sweet rolls from the bakery and a couple of bottles of beer from the grocery store. They would take turns keeping the owners busy while the other one stuffed his pockets and left in a hurry. They not only thought that was funny; they also thought it was okay because they never stole anything they couldn't eat or drink.

They said they got kind of tired being considered the "bad asses" at school, so they cooked up a plan to make others look just as bad. Sam found a couple of bottles of booze his father had hidden. One was under the old sink and the other under a pile of papers in the outhouse. There was a big sock hop planned for a Friday night. I had to ask because I had no idea what a sock hop was. They just said it wasn't anything special, just a school dance where everyone danced and hopped around in their socks, but they sure were going to make this one special. The dance always had cookies and punch; only this time the punch was going to be a little different. Along with the water and lousy jug of flavored syrup in it, there was also going to be plenty of "hooch," as Sam called it. They just wanted to see what the teachers would do when some of their "pets" got drunk.

It didn't work out quite the way they planned. Some of the kids staggered around a little, the girls giggled, and two or three got dizzy on the dance floor. One girl peed her pants, and a couple of guys puked, but Willy and Sam got drunker than any of the teachers' pets. They got drunk as skunks, started a fight with the guy who was playing the piano, and got kicked out of the hop and out of school for the next two weeks. They still ended up the bad asses but enjoyed the free two weeks so much that they decided they would like to get kicked out of school forever.

That time they had a plan that really did work. To hear Willy tell it, they walked in the classroom as bold as "Billy be shit" and started using every bad word they knew and some they made up, like "rat ass kisser" and "pig fucker." They threw erasers at the teacher, grabbed the rubber hose off her desk, and said they were going to let her see what it felt like. When she fled the room to bring in some help, they dumped lunches from paper bags, stomped all over them, and overturned some desks. Then they waited, sure that this time their plan would work. And it did. They were gone, kicked out of school forever, and as Willy said, they were as happy as "pigs in shit." Charlie's only comment was "I guess that means you are really happy assholes, because you've been kicked out of all kinds of places ever since."

One night they began telling us about other things they did. They told us about the time they tied a dog's hind legs together and rolled on the ground laughing while they watched him try to walk. And about the few times they tied cans on cats' tails and said it was real fun to see how it drove them old cats crazy. Then they told the story that they thought was the funniest tying story ever. They had tied this kid from town to a tree and told him he would stay there until the ants came to eat him alive. They said the louder he cried, the louder they laughed. They didn't think it mattered much, because everyone in town knew the kid was simple. "Cuckoo," they called him.

That was the first time that almost everyone, except Julia, left the table. Kathy left muttering something I couldn't understand, but I did understand Charlie when he mumbled, "Sick bastards." I sure got out of there in a hurry when my aunt figured out from the kitchen just what these funny stories were really all about. I was glad, because their stories made me mad and sad. The next few nights I had nightmares about dogs and cats and ants crawling all over me, so I didn't want to hear any more Willy and Sam stories. Now I spent the after-supper time listening to the radio with my Uncle Ben. Even the program "I Love a Mystery" didn't scare me the way those two did. The only time I was allowed to stay at the table, or wanted to stay there, was when it was someone else's turn to story-tell.

Kathy had some real wild stories to tell, and if any of them had been true, she would have had the most interesting life of all. She described how much she had liked eating in fancy restaurants in Paris and acted as though she was still scared to death when she told us how she had been kidnapped right off the top of a pyramid one time when she was in Egypt. She made up stories about her postcard places and trips on buses and boats, and everyone listened just as though her stories were real. My aunt told me that was the nice thing to do, so I listened. One time when I forgot it was all made-up crap, I even asked her a question. Boy, was that ever a mistake. It sent her into one of her hissy-fits, and she stomped around shouting she was never going to tell us another thing, especially me. But three nights later she was at it again.

Not much of what she shared made any sense, even to me. She could never ride a bike because one time when she was swinging, she fell off the swing and landed on an ax. She didn't go near the water because the last time she went swimming, she drowned. She said she had never gotten married because all the guys who had asked her were "real dinks." She told us that the last one who had asked her was Fish Head. He was an okay guy, but he wanted them to live with his crazy, stupid, farting old mother, so that's why she said no. Maybe that part about Fish Head was a little bit real.

She never mentioned a mother, father, or any brothers or sisters. She did mention the uncle who died because he put salt in his beer and then got hit by a train. Other than that, she only talked about her grandmother, the one who gave her the solid-gold set of silver. She said her grandmother loved her so much that she hardly ever let her go outside. She wanted to keep her real close so that some stranger wouldn't take her in the woods and chop her head off, or so that the gypsies wouldn't steal her.

A Letter from Tennessee Gets Charlie Talking

We were all excited when we got that letter from Tennessee. It gave us a break from listening to Kathy and all her crazy stories. If we had just told her to stop, she would have had a hissy fit that lasted for days, so this was just right. Even Kathy would want to know what Alice had to say. After all, she might have had a chance to go away with an apple picker if that mean old Mrs. W hadn't kept her out of the orchard night after night.

Alice wrote that she wanted to thank my aunt and Mrs. W for the kindness they had shown her and to share all the news. She had married her apple-picking husband, and they settled down. He had a steady job pumping gas and wasn't going to be on the road picking any more apples. They bought a little trailer home, and even though they had to walk across a big yard to get to the community house to take showers and do the laundry, the park they were in was still very nice, and they had a whole lot of friends. One friend even had a radio, so on Friday nights a whole bunch would get together to listen to whatever they could find to listen to.

She was pleased to tell us that she was going to have another baby. There wasn't any room in the trailer for another crib, so she was glad she had learned when she was at the boardinghouse that she could just stick it in a bureau drawer. She was also proud to report that her first child, who was more than a year and a half old, could sit up for a little while all by herself. All she or her husband had to do was prop her up in the first place. My aunt and Mrs. Walden were pleased to hear that Alice was doing well, but when they read the part about the first baby sitting up, they shook their heads, clucked their tongues, and looked sad. I either don't know much about babies or must be a really dumb kid, because I thought that was really great news.

She ended by writing that even though she was happy, she really missed us and hoped that some of us might come to visit. That really got Charlie thinking that maybe someday he just might take a little trip to Tennessee. Someday.

Charlie told us that he had been to a lot of places but somehow missed Tennessee. He said that if he did go, he could check up on Alice to see if she was really okay and maybe even bring her some things. Charlie had never talked too much at suppertime, but when Julia asked him where else he had been and why he had traveled to so many places, boy, did he open up. He had more stories than Kathy had, only his were really real. He didn't gab on about going to Egypt, but I was just waiting in hopes he'd tell us what it was like when he visited the Roman Empire.

Charlie's ma died when he was only nine years old. He had three younger sisters who also now were without a mother. This left his lonely pa in one hell of a situation. He couldn't work and take care of all the little ones without some help, so he moved in his whole family with his mother and father. Charlie said his grandparents were just the opposite of Julia's. His grandfather never had just a right way to do things; he only cared that things got done. Charlie said his grandfather was a little man who smoked a pipe, always smelled like Canadian mints, and was kind and considerate to his grandmother. He was so considerate that after a day's work, he would clean himself up in the barn with ice cold water and leave his shoes outside just so that he wouldn't drag any dirt into the house.

Charlie and his family were not the only ones to live there. His pa had a kid brother named Buddy who was the same age as Charlie, so, of course, he was there. And if that wasn't enough, he had an aunt whose husband had just run away or disappeared or something, so she moved in with her three kids. Charlie said that even with all those kids to tend to, all that laundry she had to do in a big old washtub and hang on the line, even in freezing weather, all the cooking and cleaning she had to do, he never heard his grandmother complain. She was usually smiling and was always ready to give big hugs, so all the kids knew they were loved. He had only wonderful things to tell us about his grandmother and his grandfather; it was only his pa who gave him grief and Buddy who gave him trouble.

In the beginning when they were in the lower grades together, everything seemed fine, but when they went into the high school, as Charlie said, "the shit hit the fan." He thought they really lost touch because Buddy was a big baseball star and Charlie wasn't, because he didn't have the time to try out or play. Every day as soon as school was over, he had to hurry home to help his pa. If it was winter, he had to go to different houses and help push coal from his pa's truck down the different chutes so that people could keep their stoves going. He helped cut wood, plow the snow, and, of course, harvest the ice. In the spring and in summer when school was out, he helped deliver ice for everyone's iceboxes. He'd use tongs to pick up a different-size piece of ice from the back of the truck, put it on a swinging scale to see how much it weighed, carry it into the house, tell the people how much they owed, and then take the money back to his pa. All this time Buddy did nothing.

Charlie said he really didn't feel resentful. After all, what he was doing was to help his pa. Besides, he understood that Buddy being his grandmother's last kid, the baby of the family, was probably the reason he was spoiled—spoiled in the same way only kids are spoiled. Being an only kid—that sure got my attention. I wanted to ask my aunt to get me a brother or sister real quick before I spoiled, but I never got the chance.

In school Charlie tried real hard, went to a favorite teacher whenever he need a little extra help, and got excellent grades. At the time, he was really doing it to make his father proud, but it didn't work. His pa never said, "Good job" or "Well done." He would just look at the school report, shake his head, and put it aside. Buddy, on the other hand, just seemed to drift along not caring what his report card said, and many of the other boys their age didn't even finish school. They just dropped out. I bet it was after they had time off to go help harvest the ice and liked being free and raising hell so much that they didn't want anything to do with school anymore. Getting good grades or even staying in school at all didn't seem to impress his pa one bit.

There came a time, Charlie said, when he got really tired and so discouraged that he decided to run away from home. He went to a neighboring town, snuck into the fairgrounds, and hid there for four days. Some old guy spotted him, recognized who he was, and contacted his father. Down came his pa in his truck, hopped out, and all he said was, "Time to go home, boy."

In high school Charlie not only had a favorite teacher; he also had a favorite girl named Amy. They always ate lunch together and also sat together on the front steps every recess time. This drove Buddy absolutely crazy. He did everything he could to spoil it all. If they were sitting together, he'd try to wedge his way in between them and act as if it was a big joke. He'd leave only when Amy got upset. He did everything he could think of to spoil their friendship. He even told Charlie that Amy was making a fool of him, talking behind his back, and telling everyone she really didn't like that dirty old coal guy. Charlie didn't actually believe him, but for days it bothered him, and he wasn't quite as open and friendly with Amy as he had been. It was only after Amy set the record straight and Buddy right along with it that things got back to the way they used to be.

They realized they were not only friends but were very much in love. They were certain that they could survive together no matter what Buddy or anyone else threw their way. How wrong they were! When all of Buddy's efforts seemed to fail, he had a brainstorm. It was a slick, nasty, selfish brainstorm. He went to the principal almost in tears saying he hated to have to tell something bad about Charlie, because they were really very close, but felt he had no choice. He then told his very well-thought-out lie. It was damaging and totally untrue, but Buddy was a very convincing liar. He said that during a couple of recess times, he saw Amy and Charlie out back of the school doing really bad things in the bushes. He went on sadly to say that if any of the parents found out what those two were doing on school grounds during school hours, then the principal would surely be fired. And, of course, Buddy would not want to see that happen; after all, he was really fond of the principal and thought he was doing a great job. He really laid it on thick, but, of course, all of that was pure bullshit—bullshit that the stupid principal swallowed hook, line, and sinker.

He called Charlie's pa and Amy's parents to request their presence at an urgent meeting. He was determined to take action as soon as possible because, as Buddy had warned him, his job was at stake. When Charlie's pa came to the meeting, he brought the grandmother with him. Charlie thought that because he had never been anywhere near the school, he might need his mother to show him the way in. Amy's parents sure knew the way in; actually, they were there twenty minutes early. The principal began the disturbing tale of sinful misconduct, fornication, or whatever else he could think to call it, but he never once said it was something someone had told him. He just presented it as though he had discovered it himself and it was an actual fact.

Charlie said he heard that his grandmother was very quiet during the entire meeting. He also said that for days after that, she was just sad, real sad, but he didn't think it was because of the bad things she had heard about him, but because, deep down inside, she knew Buddy had somehow been a part of this. In fact, she became extra loving to him and a hell of a lot less loving to her "baby," so he guessed she really knew for sure.

The principal, for all his outstanding moral platitudes and big-shot attitude, didn't know what the hell to do. Charlie said that at first he was going to kick him and Amy out of school the very next day, but then had second thoughts. Maybe it was because Amy's dad was the minister and had a pretty large congregation that could get upset, or maybe it was because he really was afraid of what his pa might do if he got upset, or maybe it was because graduation was only three weeks away. Above all else, he didn't want to make a mistake that would cost him his job. He informed the parents that he was going to meet with the teachers and that together they would come up with reasonable consequences. He did just that and faced a bunch of angry women.

All of the teachers liked Charlie and Amy, and very few of them trusted Buddy. Charlie's favorite teacher was the one who protested loudest: "What the hell was he thinking to bring in those parents, have a summit meeting, and cause all that trouble just because he believed Buddy and just because he was trying to cover his ass?" The principal warned her that if she continued to speak to him in such a disrespectful way, she would no longer be teaching there.

Now that the damage was done, the only thing they could think to do was keep these kids separated—no more lunches together, no more sitting on the steps at recess, no more talking to one another, and no more passing notes. They managed to monitor the situation to everyone's satisfaction—everyone, that is, except for Charlie and Amy. They were humiliated and miserable.

Graduation finally arrived. His pa didn't come, of course, but Charlie said his grandmother was there and actually stood up to applaud when he got his diploma, but not so when Buddy got his. Amy's parents were there but didn't applaud at all. After the formal graduation when folks were hanging around with their punch and cookies, Charlie's favorite teacher came to him and gave him a real big hug. When she was close to him, she whispered some good news. "Next year," she said, "all of the teachers will be back, but the principal will be out looking for a new job somewhere else." Charlie said he felt like jumping for joy but could only mutter, "What happened?" She grinned when she answered, "I don't know, but it seems as though someone got to the school board during the last three weeks and told them something, and they just refused to renew his contract."

"Wow," I thought, "that was fast." But just as Charlie always said, "what goes around comes around," and now I understood what that really meant.

Before she left, she gave him an extra squeeze and told him she would never forget him. He told her the same thing, that he would never forget her, and he never did. Just as he never forgot Amy. When Charlie reached home, he saw a strange car in his yard. It was a new little black Ford with a running board and a rumble seat. Pretty neat-looking, he said. When he asked his pa who it belonged to, without even looking at him, his pa answered, "It's yours, boy. It's yours."

What a great summer it could have been, but Charlie spent the first couple of weeks when he wasn't working driving up and down the little streets looking for Amy. He guessed everyone knew what he was doing, but no one said a thing until Buddy cornered him in the barn and began to taunt him. "What's you looking for, you dirty old coal man? Bet you're looking for your sweetie, and that's a big joke. I told you before that she was just playing you and didn't want the likes of you chasing her around. She just left town, wanted to get as far away as she could."

Charlie just up and belted him a damned good one. He had

him down on the barn floor just pounding away when his grand-mother came rushing in to break it up. Charlie said he apologized to his grandmother. He was really sorry he had gotten so angry. His grandmother took him aside and explained how violence never solved anything. She said he was a good man and should never let his temper get the best of him. I guess he listened, because even with all the ranting and raving Charlie did about unfairness, I never saw him belt anybody; he just swore a lot and swore big swear words.

His grandmother told him to sit down and listen. Amy had not skipped town to avoid Charlie. In fact, her parents had to drag her into their car. And a neighbor who was watching said Amy was just sobbing her heart out. Her parents were taking her somewhere down south to live with a relative, who they said would make damned sure she never got in touch with Charlie or he with her. It had nothing to do with the fact that he shoveled coal and his hands and nails sometimes looked dirty, or that he didn't have the best of clothes or the time to be a ball star, or that he had no mother. Nothing like that counted. The damaging part was that he was a Catholic and Amy was a Protestant. In fact, her father was the Protestant minister. It was unbelievable that Amy could even think of liking a boy like Charlie. Dating a Catholic would have brought shame to the entire family, so they took care of that.

He said he thanked his grandmother for telling him the truth. I thought he should have also found that nosey neighbor and thanked her for what she saw and what she told. I hope she had let the whole town know the real story. I guess it was bad enough to be a Catholic, but at least everyone would know it all didn't happen because he was an old dirty one.

He told his grandmother that he loved her, went outside to his car, and drove away. He didn't say goodbye to anyone—not his sisters, not his pa, and especially not Buddy.

He took three supper times to tell us all of this, but it was so interesting I really wanted him to keep going. After the third night I grumbled, saying I was really ticked off because my aunt said that enough was enough and that I had to go to bed. "Ticked off" is what I learned to say instead of "pissed off," at least when I was where adults could hear me.

Charlie was kind of quiet for a while. He did ask Julia if she wanted to ride along with him while he made one last effort to get Sadie and Shakespeare back. She agreed and willingly went. That seemed to please my aunt and Mrs. W. They thought that Julia going along was a good idea because maybe the two of them could get to be special friends. Heck, I thought they were already friends. Maybe there was something about the "special" part I didn't understand. I thought it was a good idea only because if Julia was with him, he might not use so many bad words. The last time he had a fit and swore like hell about something being unfair, he almost got arrested. He also asked Julia if she wanted to go with him to the dump just to look around. She answered with a big, loud "No!" so I guessed that did it for the "special" part of the friends deal.

Julia Continues Sharing, and So Does Charlie

A couple of nights went by, and no one told any stories. Then Sam, Willy, and Kathy tried to start in again. That's when Julia asked nicely if she could have her turn. Willy and Sam were too drunk to care, and Kathy didn't storm off to have one of her fits. She just smiled at Julia and said okay. It was a little hard for me to understand, but Julia was just like some fairy godmother or something. She made almost everyone feel nice and want to do the right thing. I sure was glad about that, but I wondered about the two old drunks. I wished she would make them disappear or turn them into crummy old pumpkins or something, but, of course, that never happened. She just kept right on practicing that tolerance thing as far as they were concerned. She sure did that much better than some of the rest of us, especially Uncle Ben.

Julia told us that she stayed with the Hendersons until she finished normal school and was overwhelmed when Lucille threw a big graduation party for her. Lucille, her preacher husband, some neighbors, and even the boys all pitched in. Julia didn't have to do one thing, not even help with the cleanup. For the first time in her life, she felt really special, like a queen or something, I guessed.

She had no problem finding a teaching job and decided that the first grade would offer the biggest challenge, and it certainly did. She always started the first day of school trying to find out what skills those little ones might already have. She asked if they could spell their names, if they knew the alphabet, could recognize numbers, and other questions like that. She said she'd never forget the one little guy who answered, "Of course not, you dumb some-of-bitch. What in the hell do you think I came to school for?"

She said there were also some others that stood out in her

memory. One day, with a little spare time and while waiting for the lunch bell, she asked if anyone had a song he or she wanted to sing or a poem to share. The first little guy got up and, with a booming voice, recited the nursery rhyme "Little Boy Blue." She thought that was a good one until she heard it all:

"Little Boy Blue, come blow your horn.

"The sheep are in the meadow and the cows in the corn.

"Where is the little boy who tends after the sheep?

"Who in the hell gives a good goddamn? I don't."

The next child came up for his turn and started to sing, "I have a fat girl in Cincinnati . . ." Julia had to stop the performance very quickly and explain that it wasn't the right kind of song for the class. The singer started to cry and said he thought it was okay because it was a song his grandfather had taught him. Did I ever wish I knew the words to that song because I bet I could even outdo Della's brothers on the playground!

She said many of the kids she taught came from difficult backgrounds, so she tried to keep that in mind as she taught them. On the first day of school one little guy came up to her desk and asked her if he could go piss. She didn't scold him or act shocked. She figured that was the only word he knew. She just very gently told him that the right way to ask was "Could I go to the bathroom?" She went through this same routine three different times with the piss thing. Then on the fourth try he simply asked if he could go to the bathroom, and she was happy as hell. She said it probably didn't seem like any big deal, but to her it was a major breakthrough.

She had other stories to tell, but one, she said, had to wait until a more appropriate time. When she said that, she glanced my way and so did my aunt, so off to the kitchen I had to go. My aunt told me to sit on the stool and wait until she told me it was all right to come back in. She said that I could have some ice cream if I wanted some or that I could go up and sit with Uncle Ben. Who wanted to sit with Uncle Ben and listen to stupid "Amos and Andy"? Not me. I didn't even want any ice cream. I just wanted to listen to what I wasn't supposed to hear and knew just how to do it. All I had to do was crawl along the hallway floor, stop just before I got to the dining room, lie real still, listen with all my might, and pray one of Mary Theresa's prayers so that I wouldn't get caught.

Julia told all those selfish grown-ups that one day after recess time when the kids came into the classroom, she noticed that one of them had written something on the blackboard. The word was *ass*. She had everyone sit on the floor in front of the blackboard and asked them, "Okay, does someone want to tell me who wrote that?"

"I wrote that," answered a kid named Ricky.

"Do you know what it spells?" she asked.

"Yes, I do," came the proud answer. "*A-s-s* spells *fuck*."

I guess they didn't want me to hear it because it had that four-letter word in it, which was silly. Fuck, fuck, fuck. The boys say it all the time at school. I even said it myself the time my aunt gave me that bug haircut!

Julia said she just talked to him about what both words really spelled and how he shouldn't ever have to use either one of them. In all of her teaching career, no matter how rough things got, she never made a kid sit in the corner, never sent him or her to the principal's office, and certainly never hit anyone with a ruler or a rubber hose.

She loved the kids, loved teaching, but sometimes really felt overwhelmed with her responsibilities. Those little kids coming into her classroom knew very little about reading, writing, and arithmetic, and there were some who knew too much about the wrong kind of things in the worlds they lived in. For ten months they would be left in her care, really be hers to teach, to direct, and perhaps even to inspire. The challenge was great, but she said over and over that the rewards were even greater.

She taught for a whole bunch of years—I guess long enough so that they would have to give her a little bit of money every once in a while so that she could eat and stuff. When she left, she said, she was looking for a nice, quiet place to settle down, and when she saw the boardinghouse, she felt it was just where she should be. Maybe the old wraparound porch and the house needing a paint job real bad made her think of the farm. Anyway, she said she was glad she had found us.

I had heard Mrs. W turn people away, telling them we were all filled up. That was because she still wouldn't let anyone move into Sadie and Shakespeare's room. Now I was sure glad that Emma kicked the bucket even before the old gentleman came looking for her, because it meant there was an empty room for Julia.

After Julia stopped talking, she just looked at Charlie, smiled her sweet little smile, and asked, "What about you, Charlie? Where did you go in that new little black car of yours?"

"Oh, hell," he answered. "I didn't really want to head south, so I just headed west." He described all the wonderful things he had seen, all the natural treasures. He described the Yellowstone National Park, the Grand Tetons, the Painted Desert, and the Continental Divide. He really got excited when he talked about them and oodles of other places, but I thought he got carried away a little when he talked about the Grand Canyon. After all, I thought, if you've seen one hole in the ground, you've seen them all.

He would travel from town to town, get a part-time job, and work until he had enough money to hit the road again. Sometimes he rented a room, and other times he just stayed with new friends he'd made. He didn't bother to keep in touch with those folks once he left but said that someday he'd love to go back and visit with them.

That would be real good for Charlie, I thought, especially if they weren't dead yet.

Julia asked if he'd found any nice girls along the way who he thought he should bring along to keep him company. At that my aunt and Mrs. W just looked at each other and grinned a little. I guess it was the way she asked it.

"There was one in Utah," he answered. "She was very nice and quite sweet. She even reminded me a little bit of Amy." But he said he sure wasn't going to ask her to join him. He had gotten into so much trouble just caring about a Protestant that he could only imagine what kind of hell would break loose if he dragged home a Mormon. There was another girl, a mountain of a girl, he said, who worked in the diner where he always had his meals. After a few weeks they became friends—not "special" friends, I guessed, but just good friends. He said he knew she really wanted to escape from that small hometown of hers, but the only problem was he didn't think her big, fat ass would even fit in the rumble seat.

He would send his family postcards every once in a while just so that they would know where he was and that he was still alive and well. The only problem was that by the time they were able to get back to him, he was already moving on, so when his grandmother died, he didn't learn about it until two months after she'd passed. Charlie was devastated, and it made him think he should probably stop all that roaming around and settle on something somewhere. After thinking things over and looking around, he decided to join the Merchant Marines.

He said that after being in that service for just a short while, he realized it was the best decision he had ever made. He became a master mechanic—and a damned good one at that. He loved the stable environment, the camaraderie, and the fact that his family could now contact him whenever they wanted or needed to. He said it was really good for him because it kept his "gasoline ass" in place. He stayed in for a little more than twenty years and left only because he felt he was needed at home. His pa had been doing poorly for the last couple of years, but now he was sick, really sick, and it looked as if a nursing home was the only answer, but it sure wasn't one his pa agreed with. Charlie remembered his father telling him more than once, "Boy, no matter how sick I get, don't let no bastard lock me up in one of them places where folks are just waiting for God to come knocking on the door."

Since the sisters couldn't convince the old man, it was clear that Charlie would have to be that bastard. Getting him to go to the nursing home was a real challenge. His pa used every excuse he could think of. He accused his kids of just trying to dump him and put most of the blame on Charlie. Finally they got him to go, but once there, it still wasn't pretty. He fought everything the home had to offer. He refused to pick something from the menu—just told them to bring whatever they wanted to, because it all "tasted like shit anyway." He refused to try any arts-and-crafts activities. He said he'd worked all his life and wasn't about to go to work for them. Once a week they had a social evening with slow music to dance by. Charlie thought that would have real appeal because his pa loved to dance and was really a good dancer. But, no, his pa wouldn't think of going, because there was nobody there to dance with except "old" ladies. After a while they all stopped trying to get him involved in anything. They just let him be, and that is exactly what he wanted.

The daughters went to visit him at least once a week, but

Charlie was there every single day. He said they just talked a little about old times and not much else. His pa told about all the people who came to visit him—the ones who didn't talk at all but just stood around his bed smiling at him. When he said just who they were, Charlie realized they were all friends or relatives who had died some time before. And then Charlie realized just what that meant. They were all there waiting for his pa because they knew that God was just about to come knocking.

After his pa passed on, whatever had sentimental value was given to his sisters. Charlie just looked for some little thing that had been his grandmother's but didn't find a thing, probably because Buddy had already gone through and taken just about everything he could get his hands on. It really didn't matter, Charlie finally said. His memories would be enough. It was while they were all milling around looking things over that one of the sisters told him about Amy.

She had come back to town five or six years before and wanted to visit with Charlie's family. She knew he wouldn't be around but wanted to find out how he was. She asked if he had ever married or had any children. Did his sisters think he was happy? Did he ever mention her to anyone? She went on and on all about Charlie. Then she shared a little bit about her life.

She had married someone of her parents' choosing and was still married to him. She never had children of her own and never felt as if she had ever been really happy. She asked that when they talked to their brother again, would they please tell him that she had really loved him years before and still did?

I couldn't wait for Charlie to talk about Amy. I was so excited I almost peed my pants. Maybe he'd say he still loved her or something. It would have been sad, but sad stories can be almost as good as funny ones sometimes, and I knew for sure that if I told it at school, at least Little Mary Theresa would cry. But all he did was hang his head a little bit, shrug his shoulders, and glance quickly at Julia. Then she smiled as if she knew something the rest of us didn't.

Nobody asked how come he had chosen Mrs. W's as the place where he would plunk himself down. I thought it was because it was close to the dump, and that way he wouldn't have too far to carry all the stuff he dug up. But Charlie said he decided that if he had a steady place to stay, it might once again help slow down that "gasoline ass" of his. It worked pretty well, except for that one time he went panning for gold.

A Stage in the Barn and a Prayer for Buster

I really enjoyed school and, with a little help from Julia, was doing very well. There didn't seem to be as many stories to tell about the boardinghouse, maybe because as I got a little older, my imagination got dull or my telling big lies made me afraid I would have to go to the priest and confess. It really didn't matter too much because there were enough true stories to make Mrs. W's still the most exciting place in town—the place where my best friends always wanted to hang out when the weekend rolled around.

My aunt told me that the boardinghouse wasn't a good place to have a lot of kids around; maybe just one guest at a time would be a good idea. That meant Della and Little Mary Theresa didn't visit with me at the same time. They just took turns. That was probably really good because they liked to do very different things. If they were there at the same time, I wouldn't know which one to please, or as Charlie would have said, I wouldn't know if I should "shit or get off the pot."

Usually when it was Della's turn, we spent half the day in the barn looking at all the junk and poking into those private boxes just looking for treasures. Then we would start trying to build a stage so that it would be ready if we ever wanted to put on a show. The last half of the day we spent putting everything right back where we found it, even Sadie's old Popsicle sticks. The stage never seemed to come out right anyway. It was always crooked and rickety, so it didn't bother me to tear it down. If we didn't think of something else to do the next time it was Della's turn, we would just build it over again. She really wanted that stage because her brothers were very excited about coming to see our show. They even had some good ideas about what we could do. Della tried to describe some of them. In one I was supposed to be the little girl mouse, and the oldest brother would be little boy mouse. It was supposed to be just like that dirty joke I told at school. After all, they argued to their sister, if we couldn't make a game out of it, we could put on a damned good show. No matter what ideas they gave Della, she said they all sounded like some kind of "you show me yours and I'll show you mine." At home the boys were always trying to show their dingle-dangles to her and her sisters, but the girls wouldn't show anything back. Now the boys were insisting that if it were a real show on a real stage, nothing would be wrong with it. They would all be just like actors, and the barn would be the perfect place. I wasn't going to get into any kind of damned mess between Della and her brothers. I was just going to make sure we never got that stage built.

When Little Mary Theresa came over for her Saturday visit, it sure was different. She loved to hang around the kitchen talking in her sweet way to my aunt and Mrs. W. Then she wanted to visit Julia for just a few minutes—just time enough to tell Julia how pretty she looked and how nice her room smelled. If Charlie was at home, she'd ask if she could come in just to admire all his dump treasures. She stayed away from Willy's and Sam's rooms, but when she got to Buster's, she did this little routine.

She had a glass bottle of water that she said was holy water. It wasn't the kind they had in church that the priest had blessed; it was just plain water that she blessed herself. First she would spread some real close to the bottom of the door, and then she would cross herself and say the same old prayer she said each time she came.

"Dear God,
"This poor old man is blind as a bat;
"He can't find his coat, and he can't find his hat.
"I am asking you to fix him, so what do you think of that?
"Amen."

Then she'd cross herself and tell me it was my turn. I'd tell her I had already said my prayer quietly and to myself.

"Dear God,
"She has made the floor as slippery as glass,
"So I pray poor Buster doesn't slip on his ass.
"Amen."

Of course, I didn't want to tell her just what my prayer was, so I crossed myself quickly. That way she wouldn't have time to ask me any questions.

Uncle Ben Wins Out—So Do We All

One Friday as I left for school, my aunt told me not to invite either one of my friends over for the next day. At first I thought I had done something wrong, or since it was Della's turn, maybe she'd heard about the show and really thought I was going to build the stage. But that wasn't it. Uncle Ben was taking the day off from work and wanted both my aunt and me to be ready for something special.

For as long as I could remember, Uncle Ben always worked on Saturdays even though it really didn't please my aunt. She thought six days a week was really wearing him out. But he'd answer only that he couldn't pass them up, that it meant double-or-nothing pay or something like that. I thought she should just be happy that he wasn't stopping by the Dirty Dozen to cheer up that Grace lady.

The three of us had breakfast together that Saturday, and even though we had the same old oatmeal and stuff, it still felt like something special. I watched my uncle, who was trying not to smile, and my aunt, who was trying not to frown or look worried. And I was just trying not to ask any dumb-ass questions. As soon as we finished breakfast, my uncle suggested we take a walk. I wondered if he just wanted to walk around a bit to make room for a little more food. God, that would have been just like Julia's pa, and I was real glad when I found out that was not what he had in mind. He said we were just to follow him as he strolled along, so we did. We followed him all the way to Becky's old house before he finally stopped.

"This is yours," he said to my aunt.

"What in the world are you talking about, Ben?"

"It's yours! This house is now yours!"

"For the good Lord's sake, will you make some sense?"

"Come here and give me a hug," he said, "and I'll tell you the whole story."

I couldn't believe Uncle Ben had asked for a hug and was even more baffled when my aunt gave him one. I had never seen them do that before, and besides, I thought they were too old for that hugging stuff, but it worked.

Uncle Ben said no one had heard from that scraggily dirty old Hank for more than three years. The house looked as if it was falling apart. The paint was peeling off, the shutters were hanging, and the grass looked like a hay field waiting to be mowed, and no one was paying the taxes. My uncle was aware of the whole mess and thought that then would be a good time to take some action. Off he went to the town hall to have a little chat with the selectmen. He told them he would pay all the back taxes and offered them a fair price for that piece of property. He reminded them that the house was in really bad shape. Where in the world did they think they could find someone else who would make them such a generous offer? The three selectmen all seemed to be in agreement when in waltzed the sheriff. He had been listening from his little office across the hall and was there to stop the whole damned deal.

He claimed he could do them one better. He knew a wealthy person who would not only pay all the taxes, but would top whatever price my uncle was willing to pay. He didn't care how high my uncle was willing to go; he would never be able to afford top dollar. The sheriff claimed this person he knew wanted that house and had more money than God. When he told us that, I wondered about the "more money than God" part. I knew that God had all the mountains, rivers, lakes, and oceans. He had the lilies in the fields and the sparrows and just about everything else, but the money part sounded fishy to me. My aunt had told me a lot of things about God, but she never once mentioned that he had even one red cent.

Uncle Ben told the selectmen that he was going back to the boardinghouse or over to the dump to find Charlie and that they were both coming back to have a nice little chat with the sheriff. I am not sure how nice that chat was, because later on almost everyone around town claimed they had heard my uncle shouting and Charlie swearing every word he knew—and even making up some new ones, like "pig fucker." It wasn't the shouting or swearing that did the trick. My uncle told us that between him and Charlie, they had all kinds of things they could hang on the sheriff that would end him for good. They would see to it that he'd never win another election for sheriff, and if they really wanted to push it, he would be damned lucky if he didn't land in jail. While my uncle was telling us this, I was really trying to picture the sheriff with "things" hanging all over him but just couldn't make it work.

Everything was settled. There were some papers to be signed, and in a couple of weeks we could move right in. My uncle knew I really liked Mrs. W's and was a little scared about moving, so he spent a lot of time with me saying how great things would be. He said there would be the big yard to play in, and he would even help me plant a garden. I would still be able to see the lake, but now it would be out my very own bedroom window, and the railroad tracks wouldn't spoil the view. I would have a much bigger bed, my own closet, and a new bureau. He promised to go to the barn and grab the other three chairs that went with my little table. He said he realized I had outgrown that set, but it would be nice to finally have all the pieces together. I could have more than one friend over at a time, and, in fact, he said a whole houseful would be just fine. He said it was supposed to be somewhat of a secret, but he knew my aunt was going to get me a brand-new guardian angel picture all my own. And best of all, he said, the house wouldn't shake when the train went by.

He laughed and asked me what I thought Emma would say if she could see me moving into a real house. But I really didn't care what Emma, my friends, or anyone at Mrs. W's would say, because Rebecca was the only one I could think about, and that's what was making me scared. I couldn't help thinking about the last time I saw her—but she sure wasn't able to see me. That scene in the parlor had kind of stuck in my head for a long time, even though I had really tried to forget the whole thing. If she could see me moving into her house, I sure hoped she didn't remember how disrespectful I had been, but if she did, I hoped she had forgiven me. After all, I was just a little kid when that happened—just a bored, curious, crazy little kid. Of course, I couldn't tell anyone that was the reason I wasn't jumping with joy about our moving, so I just made up stuff.

"If we aren't here, maybe another bum might sneak in the kitchen and hurt Mrs. W." And "Sometimes Buster needs me to help him find his way around. If we move, what will he do?" And "Charlie will be real upset if I'm not here to see all his treasures when he comes back from the dump." And "Julia won't be able to help me with my homework, and I'll flunk out of school." And "When Sadie and Shakespeare come back, just think of how upset they will be if they can't find me." All of that was for nothing. The adults at the boardinghouse didn't go for made-up stuff the way the kids at school did, so I just gave up. Besides, I thought, if Rebecca came haunting me, I could always cross myself and use the prayer that Little Mary Theresa and I made up for Old Man Walden. However, I didn't think I'd use my favorite part—"get your ass out of my home"—because that would not be a nice thing to say to a lady ghost.

Every day right after Uncle Ben left for work, Charlie got a crew together and headed over to work on the house. Willy, Sam, Julia, and even the sheriff followed Charlie's lead. The sheriff wasn't too happy to be there, and Kathy was having hissy fit after hissy fit because she couldn't be. They got the house painted and the shutters fixed, mowed that really tall grass, and Julia even planted some flowers around the yard. Everything was set, and we were ready to move in.

It really didn't take us long to pack up all our stuff, because we didn't have all that much. It would have taken longer if my aunt had let me take all the things Charlie wanted to give me, but she just told him he could bring those wonderful treasures after we got settled. Della and Little Mary Theresa said they really wanted to pitch in to help me move my clothes and stuff. They did carry a couple of boxes up the stairs to my new room but spent most of the time just nosing around. They were running up and down the hall and peeking in all the rooms and closets. Little Mary Theresa kept saying a prayer she made up on the spot: "O my dear Lord, thank you for this blessing you heaped upon my friend." Della just said a short one, "Holy shit!" over and over again, "Holy shit!" Even without their prayers, I could tell they sure were happy about me having a nice new house.

Most everything was left in the kitchen: the pots and pans, the coffeepot, the toaster, everyday coffee mugs, and most of the regular dishes. The fancy plates and all the pretty glasses and fancy napkins were nowhere to be found. Charlie said he would bet his ass that Hank hadn't taken them and would bet double his ass that we could find them either at Esther's house or with that crooked nurse Ruth. He was so upset he even volunteered to go pay them a visit and bring back a few of those things. My aunt got him to quiet down and told him he shouldn't give it another thought. She said she really didn't need anything fancy. She had plenty with just the everyday things that had been left behind. Still Charlie mumbled about the unfairness of it all. "After all," he ranted, "the house was bought 'as is,' and it sure as hell ain't 'as is' as far as I can see." Even though some of the furniture was still in the parlor, he claimed that half of the good shit was missing.

I didn't quite understand all of the "as is" stuff, but I sure was glad the piano was part of it. There it stood in the parlor, not in the same place as it was before but very close to the door. It had been moved close enough to the door that Charlie and Uncle Ben thought it had probably been on its way out. It seemed to both of them that Uncle Ben had made the deal with the selectmen just in the nick of time. They struggled to roll it back to just where it should be, and although it wasn't a real grand piano, it sure looked grand. I sat down and played just a little bit with the keys when my aunt suggested that perhaps now I could take some piano lessons from Della's mother. She made it clear that I would not be going to Della's for any lessons, but if her mother wanted to come here to teach me, she would pay her a little bit for each lesson.

I was really very excited. Not only could I learn to play the piano, but if Della's ma made a little bit of money, she could give some to each of the boys. Then maybe, just maybe, they wouldn't try so hard at shoplifting just for a stupid little fifty-cent reward.

Most every day my aunt went back to the boardinghouse to give Mrs. W a hand, and after school I would meet her there. Sometimes we ate supper there, and other times we would just walk back together and my aunt would cook something for Uncle Ben and me. I really liked that 'cause most of the suppers my aunt cooked were as good as the Sunday dinners we had at the boardinghouse.

Kathy never said anything about missing us. She just told

stories about the houses she used to live in. She went on and on about the one in England, the one in Africa, the one in Paris, and another one in Egypt. I swear she would have gone on all over the world if Mrs. W hadn't told her enough was enough.

Julia came over often to help me with my homework, and Charlie tagged along just to visit, so they didn't have a chance to miss us. Willie and Sam said that they did and that they were sorry we weren't still boarders, because they loved watching me grow up. Uncle Ben said that was another damned good reason we were out of there, because he didn't trust either one of them.

One day when I was up in my room with Della and Mary Theresa, my uncle called out to me. "Come on down," he said. "Charlie and I have something to give you." Down the three of us went, and when I saw the big box on the floor, I guessed we were settled in enough so that Charlie could bring me some of his dump treasures. But that wasn't it. When I opened the box, I saw only Rebecca's things. There were some of her books, some of her pictures of faraway places, some of her special souvenirs, some of her figurines, and tucked way in the corner was her music box—the pretty little music box I had never dared to touch.

Charlie and my uncle were grinning ear to ear, and my uncle said, "Now these things are back where they belong. Not all of them, but quite a few, so you just put them around the parlor where you would like them to be."

If I had known how to do a handstand, I would have, right there in front of God and everybody, but, of course, I didn't know how, so I just settled for jumping up and down, and my friends jumped with me. I didn't ask where they came from, because I guess I knew. The only thing I wondered was if they brought back some of the earrings for my aunt.

Mary Theresa wanted to build a shrine. Della wanted to have a sidewalk sale. I wanted to put those treasures right back where I remembered they used to be, and that's just what I did, or thought I did.

Several days went by before I noticed that things looked different. At first I was really mad at my friends for fooling around with the treasures and moving them here and there. They swore up and down that they really hadn't touched them, not even once.

Before we got done arguing, Della was swearing for real, and that sure brought my aunt running in. She told us all to quiet down and wondered what the fuss was all about. I was really in tears when I tried to explain it. All she did was look around, give me a hug, and tell me what a great job I had done. All of the things were right where Rebecca had placed them, but all three of us knew they weren't where I had put them. Now we really had to make up because we had something big and kind of spooky to talk about. We left the parlor in one big hurry, rushed up the stairs with Della in the lead, ran into my room, slammed the door, and huddled together on my bed. I didn't have to remind them of what Charlie had said about Old Man Walden moving things around his room, because we were all thinking the same thing. Rebecca was sure around somewhere!

My friends thought we should practice the prayer we'd made up when we wanted to chase the old man out of the boarding-house. But it didn't seem quite right to me; this felt a lot different. If it was Rebecca, I knew she wouldn't do us any harm. Another thing I was sure of was if we said that prayer, we couldn't use my last line: "Get your ass out of my home." God wouldn't like us saying that kind of thing to a gentle lady like Rebecca. We decided not to do anything—just, wait, listen, and stay close to one another to see if anything else happened. After a couple of weeks of a great big nothing, we stopped thinking about it.

Now I Know

My aunt told me that Charlie and Julia were coming for dinner. In the past this had always made her happy, but tonight she seemed troubled. I asked her over and over if she was all right, but she just kept moving between the sink, the stove, and setting the table. When she did answer, it was a quiet "I'm fine; I'm just fine." Even though I'm a kid, I knew that was bullshit.

After dinner I saw Uncle Ben give her a pat on the shoulder and say, "Do it, Harriet. Do it before someone else does." Then he and Charlie left to take a long walk. Julia asked me to go to the parlor and wait there for just a minute or two. She wanted to speak to my aunt, and when she was done, Aunt Harriet would come in and join me. I did what I was asked but couldn't help but wonder what was going on. Something sure was a big secret, but I knew it couldn't be that my aunt was going to have a baby. She was too old. And I thought she and Uncle Ben were probably even too old to "play nasty" much anymore. Whatever it was, I was getting plenty worried.

Grown-ups really made me mad when they told you to just wait a couple of minutes and then made you wait and wait. I was sitting there all by myself in the parlor. It seemed like forever, and I was getting madder and madder. When my aunt walked in, I forgot all about being mad; I was just plain scared. She had been crying very hard. Her nose was runny, and her eyes were all red and puffy, and I couldn't help but yell out, "What's wrong? What's wrong?" The only time I saw my aunt cry even a little was when something made her happy, like the time Uncle Ben bought me all those things for my First Communion. I think for sure she must have cried when Rebecca died and Josie jumped off the bridge, but she didn't let me see it. Now I knew what it was. I knew she was going to die just as Rebecca did, so I started to cry, "Please don't die, Aunt Harriet. Please don't."

"Come here," she said. "Sit by me, and listen closely. I am not going to die. That is not what this is all about, but it is a serious matter, so please just let me talk." She continued, "When we were at Mrs. W's and folks began to share their stories, you noticed that your Uncle Ben and I never chimed in. We stayed silent because our stories were much too private to share. Now that you are older, it is time you heard them and heard them all." She said that years earlier, after her parents died, she moved to a small Midwestern town. She lived alone in a small but really cozy and comfortable apartment and taught school. She said she wasn't as brave as Julia, so she didn't try to teach the first grade. Her choice was the second and third grades. Those were combined, but because there were only a few students, the task was really an easy one, and she loved every minute of it. She especially loved the children and could still remember most of their names and see some of their little faces. In the barn at Mrs. W's, she said, she had a chest with some treasures of her own. They weren't anything like Rebecca's, she said, but to her they were just as precious. She had homemade birthday cards, homemade Christmas cards, and oodles of valentines. There were some school pictures, and she even had a vase painted with flowers and the words, "To the world's best teacher." Someday soon she'd share them all with me.

Teachers' salaries weren't too great in those days, so she most often just fixed herself a small supper at home. Once in a while, usually on a Friday night, she'd splurge and treat herself to dinner at the local diner. That was where she met Paul. He simply slid into the booth beside her and started up a very simple but pleasant conversation. At first she wasn't sure what she should say or do, but in no time his smile really made her feel at ease. Paul was tall—more than six feet, as a matter of fact—with dark hair and olive-looking skin. She was sure I had heard the saying "tall, dark, and handsome" —well, that was Paul. He was not only very nice looking, but he also had a winning way about him, and his smile seemed to capture everyone, just as it did her.

They did everything together. They went sliding and ice

skating, took long walks, and saw every new movie as soon as it got to town. He wanted them to eat at the diner often so that she wouldn't have to worry about cooking after a long day of teaching, and on occasion he took her to a neighboring city for dinner in a fancy restaurant. One of the things Paul enjoyed the most was dancing. Hardly a Saturday went by without them going to the Silver Slipper to dance the night away. She did say that he also really enjoyed the folks standing around the edge of the dance floor watching and applauding some of his smooth moves. He was good, really good.

Even though her fellow teachers were all married and some had families, a couple of them told her that they were actually envious. They thought Paul was a real catch. He had everything any girl would want, and, lucky her, she sure was in the right place at the right time. They started dating in September right at the beginning of the school year and were together for seven months. In fact, she said, she got so that she couldn't remember her life without him. All of that changed in March. They had returned to her apartment after a night of fun and dancing, and she told Paul they needed to have a talk. She said he just answered, "You go first," so she did. She told him she loved him. He just gave her that smile of his and said he already knew that. She waited, hoping he would tell her something like that in return, but he said nothing, just kept smiling.

She had a hard time trying to decide what to do next but felt she had no choice. She didn't know what to expect but thought that out of fairness he had to be told, so she simply said, "Paul, I am going to have a baby."

"Dear God, I have to have some time alone to think about all of this" was his response. "I'm going home now but will see you tomorrow—probably breakfast at the diner."

He left without a goodbye or a smile. He didn't show up the next day, or the next, or the next. He didn't leave just my aunt; he left the whole town. She told me that she cried herself to sleep night after night and could barely function in her classroom. After a couple of weeks of all this "self pity," as she called it, she knew she would have to get back on her feet and do some serious thinking. First and foremost, *nobody* could know.

If the school board found out, she would lose her job right on the spot. They wouldn't tolerate a pregnant unwed teacher in one of their classrooms. She hoped that if she was careful, she could hide it by wearing long blouses and baggy sweaters when it became necessary. By the end of the school year, she'd be only about three-and-a-half to four months along, so that was a real possibility and exactly what she would try to do.

When her friends asked about Paul, she would tell them that he was away on a long trip but that she expected him back some-time soon. The trick was to say all that without crying or falling apart. After a while folks would realize he wasn't really coming back, but they didn't need to know any more than that. There would be a lot of guessing. Thank heaven guessing was different from knowing. But after about six weeks she realized that two people did know. One was a fellow teacher; the other was a friendly acquaintance named Ben.

The kids were all out on the playground for recess. She usually enjoyed being outside with them, but this day she just sat inside at her desk. That was where fellow teacher Marion found her. She came in, sat on the corner of the desk, and looked her straight in the eye. "I know," she said.

"But how?" my aunt asked as she tried to take a quick peek at her tummy to see what was showing.

Marion laughed, reached over and patted her shoulder, and told her that a growing stomach wasn't the only telltale sign. She had noticed that Harriet's breasts seemed a little fuller and that her mood swings were a little more pronounced, but most of all she rec-ognized a "special glow." Marion had four children of her own and was very tuned in to recognizing someone who was pregnant. She said that sometimes she knew for certain even before the mother-to-be knew. It was the glow, she said; it really was the glow.

Then she promised to help her in any way she could. She certainly wouldn't tell a soul, and if she heard any rumors, she would squash them in the bud. She was one of the older teachers and had been at that school for a mighty long time. She was respect-ed and listened to, so my aunt had no doubt she would be her chief defender and also would forever be a dear friend. My aunt said that the thing Marion told her about the glow was the most important information she had given her. It wasn't about how to keep the secret but more about how a woman looked when she was with

child. She said that all of a sudden her attitude changed. Her thinking day and night wasn't all consumed with what she would do next,
how she would raise a child as a single parent—a teacher who probably no one in any school district would hire—but now she began
to think about the little person growing inside her. She began to feel
as though she was really glowing, and somehow she knew everything would be all right.

I really wanted to ask a couple of questions. Did my aunt
think anybody could see that baby glow, or was that Marion lady
some kind of gypsy? And if my aunt really did have that baby,
where was it? I thought it would have been a cousin or something or
other of mine who must be out there somewhere. But I knew not to ask
anything just then. I'd ask when she was all done talking and sniffling.

Ben, my Uncle Ben, was the other person who knew. He
was a manager of one of the local mills and often had to travel to
different parts of the county and set up separate accounts in different cities. On one of his return trips, he saw my aunt sitting all alone
in a booth at the diner. He didn't just barge in and sit next to her and
give her a star-spangled smile. He asked if she minded his joining
her and then struggled to make even simple conversation—nothing
fun-loving or enticing. He simply asked how she was doing and
shared with her news about the mill he worked for and what his
future plans might be. It was a comfortable supper, but that was it.
A few nights later he sat with her again at the diner, only this time
the conversation wasn't quite as comfortable. He told her he knew.
He had bumped into Paul on one of his trips, and although he knew
it was none of his business, he confronted him anyway. "Are you
ever coming back?" he asked him.

Paul's answer was "Hell, no!" He went on to say how fond
he was of my aunt but that he sure wasn't ready to be a father. With
that he just smiled and walked away.

Poor Ben. It really hurt him to tell my aunt almost as much
as it hurt her to hear it.

For the next several weeks they quietly ate together. He
began to share more about himself, personal things about his past,
and he did everything he could to help her keep her spirits up. He
said a happy frame of mind would be good for the baby. There were
times when it worked, and times when my aunt would think to her-

self, "What the hell does he know?"

He knew she was going to finish out the school year but wondered what would come next. She told him she had no real idea what she would do or where she would go, and that's when he proposed. My aunt said it wasn't like a real proposal but more like a business proposition. I could just picture my poor Uncle Ben trying to fill Paul's shoes. He wasn't outgoing or lots of fun. He was a little short, not very handsome, didn't have a flashy smile, and couldn't dance worth a shit. I saw my aunt trying to teach him once, and, believe me, it wasn't pretty.

He said he could find employment just about anywhere. He asked my aunt to think about a city where she might like to live. Once she decided, he would go ahead, start the new job, and find an apartment. When the school year was over, he'd help her pack up so that she could join him. That was the deal. He told her that he didn't expect her to love him the way she loved Paul. He only wanted her to like and trust him enough to let him be part of her life. He would be there every single day caring about her and taking care of her and her little one.

She moved in with Ben in June, but they didn't marry until a few months after the baby was born. My aunt said she wasn't sure why she waited so long. I bet Ben was wondering if she was waiting for that creepy Paul to show up, but that wasn't it. She said she had real affection for Ben because of his quiet, kind, and steady ways. She guessed she just waited because she wanted to see exactly how he'd be with the baby. She had seen him around other babies, and he seemed just to ignore them, as if they weren't even worth looking at, but with this baby it sure was different.

He watched the baby every chance he had just to see if she would smile or recognize him. He held her and cuddled her, and my aunt said that one time, much to her amazement, he even tried to sing to her. That's the only time he made the baby cry, because he couldn't sing any better than he could dance, and it scared the shit out of the poor little thing. They were happy in their apartment and enjoyed certain things about city life. But after a couple of years Uncle Ben suggested there might be a better place to raise a child, and Aunt Harriet was quick to agree. She had been thinking the same thing, but Ben had done so much and seemed so settled in that she was afraid it would be selfish to suggest he go out and find something different in another location. When she agreed, he was thrilled to death and started out to try to find just the right spot.

The right spot was this town we now lived in, and a job was there for him whenever he was ready. He was even offered the opportunity to buy one of those little Dirty Dozen houses; they said he could get his hands on one with only a small bit of money down. I guess he said, "Thanks but no thanks," because he really didn't like the looks of the houses or the so-called neighborhood. He told my aunt that if we were ever going to own a home of our own, he sure as hell didn't want it to be one of those. Instead he found Mrs. W's place and assured my aunt it would only be for a short stay. I was three when we moved in, and that short stay lasted seven years.

After a couple of years went by, Ben began to try to convince my aunt that I was old enough to hear the truth. I should be told that she isn't my aunt; she is really my mother. She said she hesitated and prolonged telling me for fear it would be too upsetting. He simply asked what it would be like if someone, a person such as Emma, found out the truth and taunted me with it. How bad and upsetting would that be? She knew Ben was right but still waited until she felt the time was right. She said she finally shared her story with Julia, and it was Julia who persuaded her not to wait any longer.

So I was that baby, and all the stories about that baby were really about me. My aunt starting crying again, and I joined right along with her. I didn't know what else to do. I guess I was pissed off not because she was my mother, but because she had lied all those years. Once I quieted down, she began to explain some things we could do if I wanted to.

Everyone thought that she and my uncle were Harriet and Ben Austin and that I was their niece Emily Harriet Duncan. But we could change all that very simply. "Emily, my dear Emily," she said, "I love you so much and am so sorry that I have been deceitful. I will do whatever it takes to make you happy. You are still very young, but if you want to become an Austin, we can go to court and request an amended birth certificate. In the space that names the father, the space that has been blank for all these years, we can add Benjamin Austin. He would then legally be your father," She said so much that I was getting all mixed up and thinking mixed-up thoughts.

Didn't Uncle Ben still want to be my uncle? Would he love me any more if some piece of paper said he was my father? Would she love me any more than she already did if I started calling her Mommy or Ma instead of Aunt Harriet? Would I have to tell all my friends and teachers and everyone why, out of the clear blue sky, I had a different name? I didn't think they would laugh at me, because I'd made up so much stuff in the past, but they just probably wouldn't believe me.

I wished I were as good as Little Mary Theresa was at making up prayers, because I really did need one right then. All I could think of was to sign myself and say "amen," but if there wasn't anything in the middle, then it sure couldn't do much good. I guess just being honest with my aunt was the only way to go. So I told her, "I really don't want to do that silly court thing. I really *don't*. I am happy with things just the way they are. *Please, Aunt Harriet,* don't change anything. Let's just keep going." I told her I wasn't going to tell this story to anyone, not even my best friends, and I wasn't. She asked what I would do if someone unexpected mentioned it to me. She asked, "What if someone said, 'Hey, Emily, I know all about you,' what would you say?"

That was an easy one. I'd say, "I know all about me too, so mind your own business, asshole!"

My aunt liked that answer except for the last part. She wondered if I was curious about my so-called real father. That was an easy one, too. I now knew his name was Paul, he had a great big smile, and he danced his ass off. I didn't need to know anything more. I told her that her teacher friends who thought he was a real catch sure missed the boat. I told her the real catch was Uncle Ben! I may have been a young kid, but I did know that.

We talked for a long time and cried a little now and then. Even though I was feeling all grown up, my aunt decided she would walk me to my room, tuck me in, and kiss me goodnight. As we were headed up the stairs, we both stopped dead in our tracks. The music box was playing—it really was—and we both heard it at the same time.

It wasn't Uncle Ben who turned it on; he never would have touched something as delicate as that. It couldn't have been Julia or Charlie, because they left the house a long time ago. Tomorrow they were leaving early to head for Tennessee to visit Alice and her family. Tonight they had to pack the car with kids toys and other junk from the dump. Charlie thought they would enjoy his gifts and was also sure there were things in that pile that they probably really needed.

If it wasn't Ben, Julia, or Charlie, we both knew who it was. It was Rebecca!

In my room I told my aunt about the figurines being all in the right place and that I hadn't done that. She was sure they were back where Rebecca wanted them to be. I could understand that, but why would she play the music box all of a sudden? "It was to give us peace. She wants us to know that she thinks we have made the right decision to go on loving each other just as we have in the past." My aunt also told me that she thought Rebecca was pleased as punch that we were living there. We were filling this old Victorian with love—something that had been missing since the day she moved in.

I hoped Rebecca would really stay around. I felt as if she was more of a guardian angel than the one in the picture hanging over my bed.

Epilogue

We soon learned that Charlie and Julia were not coming back right after their visit to Tennessee. Charlie reported that Alice was doing fine. He also told us that her second child was much bigger and brighter than the first one she had. In fact, he said the youngest one was teaching the older one some really neat things, like how to crawl and even to say a word or two. But mainly he was satisfied that Alice was happy and safe. Now they were going to keep moving on, going to see some of the old friends he had met in his earlier travels.

Aunt Harriett said it wasn't just to renew friendships but to show off Julia, to let his old friends know he had finally found the someone special he had been looking for over the years. I hoped they wouldn't be away too long, because if I didn't have any more boardinghouse stories, I would need some of Julia's jokes to keep me in a star's position on the playground.

Mrs. W had some new boarders for our old rooms. It was a man, his wife, and their little girl. She said she was very happy because it filled the void that was there after we left. I really hoped the little girl would learn to love Mrs. W's just as I had. Kathy, on the other hand, just wished they would move the hell out.

Willy and Sam still got into trouble every once in a while— not enough to land them in jail but enough so that when people saw them headed in their direction, they locked their doors or stepped aside to avoid them.

Buster was still blind and alive, so Della's brother who made fun of him and taunted him wasn't blind yet.

In a few days a new school year would start, and I was really excited. I had a new project for my best friends. I would tell them about the "glow" and say I had read about it in an old gypsy book I found somewhere. I just hoped they didn't ask me exactly where, because I would have to tell another lie. Here was the plan: We were going to watch all our teachers closely to see if we could tell which one might be going to have a baby. We couldn't tell by the size of the tummy, because they might be able to hide that; and we couldn't tell if their tits were getting bigger, because sometimes some of them wore bras that were stuffed with something or other; and we sure couldn't tell by mood swings, because some days the teachers would be happy and full of fun and on other days they would be real bitches. That left us with only "the glow." I gave some lessons to Della and Little Mary Theresa on what to look for, even though I didn't know myself. But whatever I told them sure sounded good, and, of course, because I was their leader, they were more than willing to believe me. We were all set to start our new adventure as soon as the school doors opened.

That is pretty much it. We went on as usual, all of us. Nothing changed for Aunt Harriet, Uncle Ben, or me. Della and her sisters still didn't have a cot in their bedroom, and the chickens still roamed around inside. One of her brothers did get arrested for shoplifting, but her pa bailed him out and told some big, sad lie, so nothing much happened. Little Mary Theresa, her mother, and brothers just kept doing the same things: praying a lot and kneeling on beans when it was time to do penance. The brothers were still helping to serve the Mass, and Little Mary Theresa was still helping to serve the beans.

The world just kept going on just like always, and so did we. Amen!